On The Other Hand

CW01082433

Pavol Rankov **On The Other Hand**

Translated by Magdalena Mullek

TERRA **LIBRORUM**

Terra Librorum
London

Copyright © Pavol Rankov, Elpeka s.r.o. 2022
Translation copyright © Magdalena Mullek, 2022

Edited and proofread by Jamie Lee Searle, Eleanor Updegraff,
    Linden Lawson
Cover design by Mimi Wasilewska
Typeset by Mimi Wasilewska

LITERÁRNE
INFORMAČNÉ
CENTRUM

This book was published with a financial
support from SLOLIA, Centre for
Information on Literature in Bratislava

ISBN 978-1-914987-04-5
ISBN 978-1-914987-05-2 (EBOOK)

Printed in Poland

All rights reserved.

No part of this book may be reproduced, stored in a retrieval system,
or transmitted in any form or by any means, electronic, mechanical,
photocopying, recording, or otherwise, without the prior written
permission of the Publisher.

www.terralibrorum.co.uk

Contents

To Shoot Dogs

The present-day combination of the annulment of entry
visas and the reinforcement of immigration controls
has profound symbolic significance. It could be taken
as the metaphor for the new, emergent, stratification.
(Zygmunt Bauman, *Globalization*)

Their cohabitation began when Blanka moved in with
Pietro in Turin. Not the cohabitation of Blanka and Pietro,
but that of Blanka and Antoinetta. Blanka only lived with
Pietro after dark. He came home from work around seven,
they ate dinner together—Blanka mostly fed him salads
because they couldn't be overcooked or burned—then,
in keeping with Pietro's bachelor habit, they lay in bed,
watched a *totalmente stupido* TV show, the kind only one
of Berlusconi's channels could broadcast, such as celebrity
news and gossip, in which bleached-blonde *veline* in bikinis
hung on ropes like props. The host of the show would occasionally tap one of their heads with his index finger and
proclaim that it was completely hollow. The people in the
studio found it extremely funny. Pietro did too. Blanka
didn't even know how to translate the word *velina*.

In the morning Pietro usually got up when Blanka was
still asleep, made her breakfast—which is to say he pulled

a yoghurt and a juice out of the refrigerator—and woke her up with a goodbye kiss. He was in a hurry, because he always wanted to get to the *agenzia* first in order to keep tabs on his subordinates. At the beginning Blanka kept asking him to wake her when he got up, but Pietro didn't want to. He laughed, saying that when he had been Blanka's age he could also sleep until noon, and he hated anyone who ruined it for him. And since he didn't want Blanka to hate him, he let her sleep.

Antoinetta got there around ten. The first few days she caught Blanka in her pyjamas. Blanka felt really awkward when Antoinetta passed by her with a mop or the vacuum cleaner, or when she stirred up dust over her head with that odd, nonsensical device which looked like it was made of peacock feathers. It made Blanka feel like a sponger, an exploiter tormenting the poor proletarian woman who relied on the couple of hundred euros that Pietro paid her for cleaning the apartment.

'I don't want us to have a servant,' Blanka said to Pietro after she met Antoinetta for the first time.

Pietro gave Blanka a look of surprise, as if he didn't understand her broken Italian again. Then he started to explain the difference between the words *serva*, a servant, and *domestica*, a housekeeper. Palaces and castles have servants, but every rationally thinking member of the upper-middle class has a housekeeper.

'Upper-middle class,' Pietro repeated in English.

'It's…' Blanka ran to get a dictionary, '…demeaning,' she said when she found the right word.

Pietro raised his eyebrows, entertained.

'It's demeaning to Antoinetta,' Blanka went on. 'She's cleaning our dirt. A twenty-five-year-old Slovak woman makes a mess, and she, a worn-out fifty-year-old Italian *signora*, has to clean it up.'

Pietro burst out laughing.

'But that's her job. She's an expert on dirt. When my TV breaks, I call a professional; when I want a new tiled floor, I call a professional; and when I want to have a clean house, I call a professional.'

Pietro thought for a minute, then added:

'This is how it works under capitalism: everyone does what he knows how to do. You'll see, some day it'll be like that in Slovakia too.

'And most importantly,' Pietro raised his index finger, 'don't look at it from an ethnic perspective. It's not a young Slovak woman versus an old Italian woman. You can be sure that our cleaning lady, who works for three or four households, makes more money than your mother, who is a physics professor in Bratislava.'

Blanka protested some more, saying that she could clean the toilet herself—in fact, she wouldn't even have to wear the funny pink rubber gloves that Antoinetta wore while doing it—but when Pietro proclaimed that his future wife would be taking care of the children and not the household, she finally gave in.

Next came a brief period of Blanka's attempts to befriend Antoinetta. She opened them with 'homely' topics, for example by trying to explain that people ate a lot of meat in

Slovakia. Antoinetta looked her up and down with disgust, and asked whether things were really that bad in Romania.

'Not Romania,' Blanka corrected her, 'Slovakia.'

Antoinetta sighed, nodded understandingly, sprayed a thick layer of blue foam on to the stove, and carried on with her work. It wasn't until that night that Blanka realised she had confused the word *carne* with the word *cane*. *Carne* meaning meat, *cane* meaning dog. She had told the cleaning lady that Slovaks ate a lot of dogs. Pietro was quite entertained.

When Blanka tried to explain to Antoinetta the next day that in her country people didn't eat dogs but meat, the *domestica* just waved her hand.

'Over the last few years, many such,' Antoinetta used her fingers to slant her eyes, 'have moved into our neighbourhood, and people say they also eat dogs. Maybe it's good for you.' She laughed.

From that point on, Blanka's conversations with Antoinetta took the form of language lessons.

'*Il detersivo per il bucato.*' Antoinetta pointed to the laundry detergent.

'Il detersivo per il bucato,' Blanka repeated humbly.

'*La polvere.*' Antoinetta ran her finger through a layer of dust on an armoire.

'La polvere,' Blanka agreed.

On another occasion Antoinetta grabbed Blanka's arm with her rubber-gloved hand and led her to the bedroom. With a swift motion she lifted the covers, and her pink finger pointed to a stain on the sheet.

'*La macchia.*'

Blanka ran out of the apartment and didn't come back until the afternoon, when she could be sure that Antoinetta was long gone. The vacuum cleaner was standing in the middle of the hallway, waiting for Blanka, and a piece of green paper was taped next to it on the tiled floor with the word *l'aspirapolvere* and a large arrow pointing unmistakably at the vacuum cleaner.

One Sunday, when Pietro and Blanka were having lunch at a restaurant and had time for a longer conversation, the second offensive against the cleaning lady began. Blanka described various situations from their cohabitation, trying to explain her feelings. Pietro was mostly silent, which gave Blanka hope that this time he was really considering her words and taking them seriously.

When he finished his last bite, he gave a satisfied nod and said:

'Now let's set all emotion aside. Give me one rational argument, and I'll terminate her contract tomorrow.'

Blanka was silent, as much taken aback by Pietro's ignorance as by the fact that there was a contract between a cleaning lady and a homeowner. The roar of the scooters the Italians so loved to ride streamed through the restaurant windows from Via Pietro Micca.

'Buy me a Vespa,' Blanka said. 'While Antoinetta's cleaning, I'll go and ride around town.'

'That would be quite risky. A cop could stop you at any point. Until we're married, your stay in Italy isn't completely legal. We could end up having problems. They'd question the neighbours; they might even bother people at my company. They'd try to make you out to be a prostitute.'

But then Pietro smiled.

'I know what you can do to get out of the house while Antoinetta's cleaning!'

'*Grazie*,' Blanka thanked him, half sarcastically. But Pietro didn't detect any sarcasm. He leaned over and kissed his young lover, perhaps too passionately for his age.

Pietro was one of those managers who only promised what they could deliver. The sooner the better. This good habit carried over into his private life as well. On Monday he left the office right after lunch. He headed to the animal shelter and picked up the first dog that fitted his requirement of being small and cuddly. That was how he introduced the dog to Blanka.

'*Piccolo e affettuoso.*'

Blanka was speechless when she saw the ferociously barking Chihuahua. Pietro spouted all the instructions he'd been given at the shelter about feeding, hygiene, and vaccines, and then he considered the matter closed.

'I'm curious what Antoinetta will say tomorrow when she finds out she'll be cleaning up after a dog too.'

'She won't say anything; she's a professional, you'll see. Instead you should think about a name for the dog.'

'Antoinetta,' Blanka exclaimed.

Pietro laughed. 'That won't work, it's not a female dog.'

'Then Antonio!'

'Toni? That has a nice ring to it. Toni, quiet! Toni, stop barking!'

The next morning Blanka stayed at home. She waited for Antoinetta so she could explain to her that the dog, which would be making all kinds of messes around the house, was Pietro's idea—*il padrone*'s, not hers. And that was how she put it to Antoinetta.

'At least you won't be so lonely here all day,' Antoinetta said, praising Pietro.

From then on, Blanka took off for a walk with Toni right before Antoinetta's usual arrival time. Sometimes they ran into one another in the stairwell, but the dog really proved to be a useful tool for limiting encounters with the cleaning lady. Outside was another matter. Spending two hours outdoors with Toni before the cleaning lady left required incredible effort. Blanka had never paid any attention to the dogs that lived in their neighbourhood, but she quickly figured out that they were big, definitely much bigger than her Chihuahua. Bull terriers, pit bulls, and Dobermans from the area ferociously picked on the small interloper. The owners could barely keep them on their leads, so they at least made themselves feel better by yelling at Blanka to keep her dog from barking so much, because it was provoking the other dogs. Blanka didn't know what to do. Every time she met another dog, she picked Toni up to calm him down and protect him from his large adversaries, which even she was afraid of. Toni kept scratching and flailing in Blanka's arms, trying to free himself; he wanted to be on the ground. Blanka didn't know whether he wanted to fight the dangerous opponents or run away from them. In her mind it was only a matter of time before they'd run into a German shepherd or a Rottweiler that was not on a lead. The big dog would jump on the Chihuahua and chew it to bits. Oddly enough, when she told Pietro about it, he took her seriously.

'I know what we'll do,' he said, pulling down a small box from the top shelf of the wardrobe in the hallway. Blanka watched him, curious, but the item he pulled out of the box took her breath away.

'*Pistòla.*' Pietro beamed.

'Why do you need that?' Blanka asked in a choked-up voice.

'I haven't needed it so far, but I know what I'll do with it this weekend. We'll go for a walk with Toni, and if some dog attacks him, I'll simply shoot it. It'll be a warning. The other owners will hear about it, and they'll leave you alone.'

'You'll end up in prison,' Blanka whispered. Ever since she had seen the pistol, she was afraid to speak out loud, as if someone were eavesdropping.

'Don't worry, I own the gun legally. It's precisely for Situations when I'm in danger. We'll say that the dog attacked us, not Toni. *Non c'è problema.*'

'But you were telling me I should avoid cops,' Blanka said, but Pietro just waved her off.

Blanka didn't agree with the whole crazy idea, and on Saturday she checked Pietro twice before they left the apartment to make sure he didn't have the gun with him.

On top of the problem called Antoinetta, there was now another problem called Toni. The fear of meeting the cleaning lady was replaced by the fear of meeting large dogs. Toni must have been stressed out as well, because he kept barking more and more. Thankfully, he spent most of the time in the apartment asleep, so there was peace and quiet, but outside he barked practically non-stop.

By accident, which sometimes happens when you most need it, Blanka discovered Parco del Valentino. The park was empty in the mornings, except for a retiree whom Blanka saw every now and then sitting on a bench, warming himself in the sun. With her barking dog on a lead, she gave everyone a wide berth. She even developed the ability to ignore Toni's noise, so her walks in the park were very calming. Life in the apartment cleaned by Antoinetta became quite bearable.

But as is usually the case with happiness, Blanka's didn't last long. One day she met Antoinetta in the park. She wouldn't even have noticed her, but all of a sudden Toni started to bark happily and dragged Blanka across the lawn with unprecedented strength.

'*Tonino mio.*' The cleaning lady was so happy to see the dog that she picked him up.

'What are you doing here?' Blanka asked, dumbfounded.

'I live nearby, on Via Nizza. I just have to cross the park and I'm home. I walk through here every day, and if you come here regularly as well, it's strange we haven't run into each other before. Isn't that right, my dear Tonino?'

When Antoinetta put the dog down, Blanka wanted to say goodbye quickly and leave.

'*Aspetta un momento*,' the cleaning lady said. 'I must warn you. This park is a very dangerous place for a young woman like you. You shouldn't come here! Local criminals gather here. The place is teeming with immigrants.' With a familiar motion Antoinetta slanted her eyes. 'A bunch of Romanians, you know the kind I'm talking about… They murder, rob, rape, and sell drugs to our children. The *carabinieri* should shoot them like dogs… Indeed, Torino is not what it used to be.' Antoinetta sighed.

Of course, the warning didn't dissuade Blanka. She kept going to the park as before, she just avoided the pavement where the possibility of meeting the woman she despised loomed.

I know that Blanka will keep going there. I expect that after our meeting she'll go to more remote areas of the park where people don't go.

It's just a matter of time. I'll find her either today or tomorrow, the day after tomorrow at the latest. These Romanian prostitutes are so predictable.

Only our Italian men with their brains in their pants don't see through them. They can't seem to understand that the only thing those bitches want is to marry a serious Italian in his prime. Soon she'd start cheating on Pietro, then she'd divorce him and take half of his possessions. He'd end up old and alone.

Those bitches should be shot, all of them, one after another. I know I won't make a big dent, but at least I'll rid our poor Torino of one of them. I'll put the barrel to her head and shoot. Then I'll press the pistol into her hand. In the evening they'll say on the news that an illegal immigrant of questionable reputation has shot herself with her lover's gun.

I'll buy myself new rubber gloves and remove all the stains from my dress. When it comes to eliminating dirt, I'm a professional.

Us and Them/Them and Us

Those people were different from us. It was as if they didn't even want to be in charge of their own fate. They were resigned, but I wouldn't say that they were meek. I got to know them fairly well and, in my opinion, they sincerely believed that everything would go back to the way it had been, and the entire nine-year war would disappear like a bad dream after the alarm goes off. They weren't passive; it was more of a suppressed impatience, an expectation that any minute now the thing that was supposed to happen would happen. All they would do was mess it up, so it was best to wait.

The women spent most of their time with their children. I think that during the time they were with us, we had created a pretty good environment for them to play and learn.

The men were always sitting in the rec room, listening to the news. When the news ended on one channel, they switched to another. Every now and again one of them would shout out, as though he had seen something that affected him personally. Their small country appeared frequently, so it was quite possible that they had caught a glimpse of a familiar person or place. Despite reopening old wounds, the constant sitting in front of the television also had a positive effect—the men were improving their language skills. They had learned the military and political jargon of our language so well that they were mixing some of our words into conversations in their native tongue.

Something that happened on the night before their departure has stuck in my memory. I was in the middle of handing out dinner (they received pre-packed meals on Mondays, Thursdays, and Sundays). I kept hearing the disinterested voice of the news anchor, who was talking about what was going on in their country. He said that a new chemical weapon had been used, and it was going to have long-lasting effects. Then I heard English. An American military expert was explaining that the affected area would be uninhabitable for fifty to seventy years. He talked about the chemicals in the weapon, but that was beyond me. I have no doubt that this piece of news was the reason the men didn't pick up their dinner that night.

***

It wasn't easy. In my role as the representative of the refugees I had learned to understand the way they think. Let me clarify: I didn't understand them, but I could predict their reactions, even if their motives remained unclear to me. They interpreted every change we asked them to make as yet another defeat. And I was supposed to stand in front of them one evening and tell them that the next day at noon they'd be taken away on buses. When I turned off the television and started to explain the reasons, I felt like I was lying to them. Of course, what I was saying was completely true—the number of refugees in our region had increased so much that we had to adopt a complex solution—but their eyes were saying that I was a liar. The helplessness with which they watched me refuted all my arguments. Those men (naturally, the women were not present) nodded their heads in understanding, but in reality they were desperate. I'm sure that many of them recognised the name of the city where they were to be taken the next day from history textbooks, but they didn't ask any questions.

Their silence forced me to keep talking. I explained that in the front part of the complex there was a museum, which would remain open. They would be housed at the back, in the army barracks that had been there for several decades. The housing was better than what we could offer here, and the families would have at least a modicum of privacy. Truth be told, they had been living like paupers in this school. Yes, I used the word paupers. It slipped out, because I couldn't come to terms with their resigned silence. They could have said that they didn't want to be relocated to such an awful place, and I would have called off the next day's transport. I would have delivered their petition directly to the minister. I would have explained to him that these people had come to us because they believed in our humanity. We should respect them precisely because they had chosen our country as a refuge from war.

But the men didn't utter a single objection.

***

We put up the lists on the bus doors. They walked from one bus to another, looking for their names. Then they picked up their luggage (it was interesting to see how little some of them had), and they got on. They were calm and organised. I was therefore surprised when I found out right before our departure that one of them was missing. An old man who had been pottering around me the whole time explained that the missing boy had escaped during the night. No one knew where he had gone.

When I called the police, I could barely pronounce the refugee's name, and I'm sure the sergeant wrote it down incorrectly.

***

After only four days, the barracks were filled to more than fifty per cent capacity. It was a hectic time for me. The major was spending most of his time with them, so I had to hand down decisions: the kind a secretary not only doesn't make under ordinary circumstances, but ones which she isn't even allowed to make. I gave orders about the furniture that was being delivered, about sewer repairs, and about painting.

The barracks, which I couldn't picture in any other way than grey-green army tedium, turned into yellow-and-pink kitsch overnight. It was one of the major's typical ideas— if it's not going to be green, it might as well not look like a barracks at all.

After about a week, the major decided to welcome them via the PA system. But what can be said to people in their situation? First, he informed them about their living arrangements. As if they didn't already know that there were two to three families per room, that breakfast was in the morning, lunch was at lunchtime, and dinner was in the evening. Then he talked about the new weapon (because the administration had decided to use this news as an excuse for relocating the refugees here). Its effects would be long-lasting, therefore our government was looking for a multi-year solution.

***

It was an insignificant incident involving a few individuals, and it had nothing to do with relationships between entire groups of people. I would certainly not call it a conflict with the local citizenry, as the papers put it.

A few youngsters from the barracks (or, as it had come to be known, the camp) had gone out dancing. They were interested in the local girls, but the local boys didn't like it. They didn't even get in a fight. Maybe they shoved each other a few times, but that was it. The guys from the camp quickly backed off, and the locals didn't bother pursuing them.

The next day, when I was on duty at the gate, a few loud--mouthed adolescents showed up (I recognised them, because back when this was still the barracks, our soldiers had had run-ins with them in town). We called the cops, and the whole thing was over in ten minutes. The first article appeared in the papers ten or twelve days later.

The major's reaction really surprised me. Restricting their outings to the morning hours seemed disproportionate. I expected that after the announcement half the camp would show up at the gate to defend their rights. But they accepted the restriction as a matter of course.

***

In a conversation with the minister I pointed out that their demands were really minimal. Their only larger request was that we set up a house of worship for them. We should have thought of it ourselves. The minister gave me a dirty look, and I immediately tried to backpedal. I was the one who should have thought of it. I wasn't trying to criticise him, only myself. I tried to say that it fell within my purview, but he looked offended throughout the rest of our meeting. It was one of those situations that confirm my notion that soldiers should only report to soldiers. Civilians have way too many emotions and considerations—especially when it comes to their own person.

***

The nurse repeated several times that this measure applied to all the children without exception. Supposedly, an epidemic had broken out among the children in sector B or C, and its symptoms were fever and diarrhoea. Two children had died, and the camp administration had to prevent further tragedy. Until the danger of infection passed, the children would be isolated in the newly built sector L, where they would be well cared for. There would be several doctors on site and the most up-to-date equipment. Moreover, the camp administration was planning to start a regular education programme.

I didn't dare tell the nurse, but I think the epidemic was caused by food. It's been getting more and more disgusting. Sometimes I get the sense that they're using us to test the digestibility of new substances and products.

***

I think that the lockdown was the right thing to do. After all, the infection could have been brought in from town. Conversely, it would be very unpleasant if the disease spread from the camp to the surrounding areas. For now, the locals are tolerating us very well, so we have to work hard not to cause them any trouble.

I do hope the kids get well soon. I feel sorry for their mothers. The poor women don't even know how their sons and daughters are doing. There are rumours that several children have died. Someone needs to ask the camp administration to keep us better informed.

***

I don't believe a word they're saying. I'm sure that the whole story about sex orgies in sector H is made up. It's just an excuse to separate the men from the women. I don't know what they got out of forcing us to move in a matter of minutes.

With each passing day there are more soldiers here. Yesterday I talked to several other men about it. They've noticed the same thing. When we got here, we didn't see any uniforms; now they stand guard on every corner. I understand that their assignment is to cordon off the men's sector from the women's sector, but since I consider this separation pointless and unnatural, I don't agree with their presence.

***

They really don't have to apologise to us for the shooting in the distance. The camp director was assuring us via the PA system that it's regular army training, which continues to take place at this facility, even though the barracks have been moved. No problem, let there be training. None of us mind, and we don't think anything of it. Except for the couple of morbid jokes that started to circulate about the shooting.

I hardly ever hear the shots. I'm more interested to know when I'll get to see my daughters. They're still in the children's sector. No epidemic lasts this long.

They should also tell us whether the soldiers are allowed to use violence. I acknowledge that the woman in question tried to break the rules and slip into the men's sector, but that's no reason for hitting or kicking her.

***

The director tried to sound authoritative, but I could hear his voice shaking. He must have been nervous, because it was the first time that the whole camp was lined up in front of him. He had never seen the enormous human mass which was subordinated to him.

The news that we'll start working the following week made most of us happy. It goes without saying that we want to save up for when we can start a new life. But he could at least have told us how much we'll be paid. If they charge us for food and housing, it probably won't be much.

In any case, at least it gives us some hope for the future. It would be amazing to live with my wife and children again, out in the world.

**

The director is a strange man. He forces us to do things we don't want to, but then he asks our consent for obvious things that are sure to make everyone happy.

That's what happened this time. We were to decide whether we wanted new clothes. Of course we do. We don't care that we'll all be dressed the same. All we need are sturdy, warm overalls, which won't fall apart while we're working.

**

There's nothing worse than getting sweaty while working and then catching a chill during roll call in the cold rain and wind. Three roll calls a day are exhausting for us, and needlessly taxing for them.

Even so, I like the wind. At least it carries away the nauseating smoke from the large chimney at the front of the camp. They say it used to be a museum.

New Mankind

> And Zarathustra spoke thus to the people: 'I teach you
> the overman. Man is something that shall be overcome.'
> What is great in man is that he is a bridge and
> not an end; what can be loved in man is that
> he is an overture and a going under.
> Friedrich Nietzsche, *Thus Spoke Zarathustra* (1883)

She stepped down on to the dirty asphalt of the railway platform. In one hand she held a large suitcase, in the other a hanger with a black dress she was planning to wear to the funeral. And then it dawned on her that she had no idea how she was going to do it. She didn't have the keys to her brother's apartment, and it wasn't a given that they'd hand them to her at the hospital. Her brother could have left them with a neighbour who would water the plants. It wasn't out of the question that she'd end up at a hotel.

She concluded that it made no sense to drag the dress and the suitcase with her. She left them in a luggage locker at the train station. She'd go back for them in the evening.

There was a taxi stand right outside the station. She got into the first available car, and before the taxi driver could turn to her she said:

'To the oncology clinic, please.'

The doctor silently shook her hand. Then he motioned for her to sit down in the armchair across from his desk.

'How could he have died so suddenly?' she asked.

Those were the first words spoken between them, and they may have come out harsher than she had intended. She thought she caught a glimpse of anger on the doctor's face. Then he gave a resigned sigh and responded in a monotone, official voice.

'He didn't die suddenly at all. His condition was hopeless for weeks. There was no dramatic decline to speak of. Your brother had been gradually *nearing* death for a long time...'

'I didn't know that,' she whispered.

'We didn't know that you didn't know. Normally, relatives enquire about a patient's condition,' he said, suppressing any hint of a spiteful tone. But his look revealed how curious he was to see the effect of his words.

He had achieved his desired outcome; the young woman in front of him went on the defensive.

'He called me regularly, but he never complained,' she said, faltering.

The doctor gave a pensive nod.

'He wasn't one to complain. By the end he must have been in a lot of pain, but he didn't so much as wince.'

Then, as though remembering his role, he quickly added:

'We were giving him strong and effective painkillers.'

'The last time he called me was on Tuesday...' she said, still stunned.

'Last Tuesday?' the doctor interrupted her. 'He couldn't even sit up in bed by himself. He could barely hold a book.'

'On the phone he told me that he was getting ready to go home for a few days.'

The doctor raised his eyebrows, taken aback, and shook his head. It wasn't clear whether he was shocked by the words of the now-deceased patient, or by his sister who was sitting in the armchair across from him.

The doctor explained that the body had already been transferred to the pathology department in the basement. But they were only open in the mornings, so there was no point in her going there. They wouldn't let her in anyway. She should only go there once she'd arranged a date for the funeral, to let them know when the body of the deceased should be delivered to the cemetery.

An old nurse came to the door with a large white plastic bag.

'This is everything,' she said.

'What do you mean—*everything*?' the sister of the deceased asked.

'We can check it together, if you'd like,' the nurse said, sounding defensive.

'That's not what I meant,' she said, and hurried to explain: 'Please understand. I don't want to take home… things like his toothbrush, slippers, and such. Is there anything… hmm… personal, that would remind me of him?'

'Right on top is that *book* of his,' the nurse answered in a conciliatory tone.

The woman peeked into the bag, then practically shouted:
'That's the one I bought him.'

An encouraging smile appeared on the old nurse's lips.
'His head was constantly buried in it. He must have read
it several times.' She hesitated briefly, wondering whether
to go on, but then she continued. 'When he could barely
move any more, he'd stare at a page for an hour. Then he'd
push the button to call me to turn the page.'

'Did he suffer?' she asked. 'The doctor told me he was
in a lot of pain.'

'He didn't suffer at all. It was as though he was already
living somewhere else, maybe in that book, and not here at
the clinic,' the nurse said, and opened the door, revealing
a long hallway lined with two rows of closed doors.

The nurse looked back.

'Sometimes I encounter this sort of a thing with religious
patients... But he wasn't religious, was he?'

'Probably,' the young woman blurted out, and put the
book into the large plastic bag. She didn't know herself
whether her *probably* meant *probably yes* or *probably no.*

She stood on the threshold of his apartment. As if she were
waiting to see whether her brother wouldn't come to greet
her after all.

For the time being she left the door to the stairwell open.
She told herself that she had left it open to air the place
out a little while she opened the windows. The draught
slammed the door shut immediately anyway.

The apartment was small. A small entryway led to a small

kitchen, a small bedroom, and a large bathroom, which was actually also small, since the toilet was in the same space.

The ficus in the entryway had dried out. There was a thick layer of dust on the furniture. She walked into the kitchen.

'That's impossible,' she whispered, looking at the counter.

On it was a rock-hard lemon half and a jar of honey, which had crystallised into sugar. She had forgotten them in her morning haste when her brother had been hospitalised for the first time. On that occasion, she had stayed in the apartment for two days. On the last morning she'd run to the hospital to see him before her train's scheduled departure, to give him a book she had bought the day before. A few days later he'd called her. He'd said he was back home. When she apologised to him for the lemon and the honey she had left on the counter, he'd just remarked that she used to do the same thing every day when they were children, and he had got used to it long ago.

But her brother *hadn't been* home since then. Not once. There were no repeat hospitalisations; he had remained in the hospital continuously. Now it made sense why the doctor had been so reserved with her that morning. Her brother had been in the hospital for five months, and she'd never come to see him.

She only visited him right at the beginning. It was about a week after he was taken into hospital. He called her and told her his diagnosis. She showed up the next day. He seemed calmer than his voice had made him sound on the telephone. He said he'd be getting radiation therapy, followed by chemo. Supposedly the doctors didn't consider his condition hopeless at all. Her brother's words sounded so reassuring that she gladly believed them. She didn't ask the doctors about anything.

That day her brother sent her to a nearby bookshop to get a book that had been lent to him briefly by another patient who had shared his room at the beginning of his hospital stay. But the patient had been sent home, and her brother hadn't been able to finish the book.

The bookshop was just a few steps from the hospital. Its interior gave her pause. A low ceiling, a narrow staircase, dated furnishings. Mutants, robots, aliens, and muscular supermen scowled at her from the dust jackets on the shelves. She realised that the young salesman was looking at her, puzzled. It must have been obvious that she *didn't belong* there.

'I'm looking for *New Mankind* by Jerry Howland Jr.' She read the title of the book off a piece of paper. The salesman wrapped the book, and when he told her the price she was momentarily stunned by how expensive books were even in this hovel.

Now her brother had been dead for twenty-four hours, and she was sitting with the book in her hands. She had yet to muster the courage to pull the other things out of the plastic bag.

Jerry Howland Jr.: *New Mankind.* On the cover was a drawing of a man with a smaller person scrunched up inside his body. Even as she was buying the book, its cover had reminded her of pregnancy brochures.

She didn't find the first sentences of the novel at all interesting. They were actually annoying. The whole first page was. And the second one.

Once in a while she read books, but she did so for rest and relaxation, and works such as the one she was holding definitely did not provide that. The most surprising thing was that this sci-fi novel—though judging by the first pages, more of a psychological novel—had garnered her brother's interest. For years she had been convinced that her brother never so much as touched a book. The furnishings of the apartment she was staying in confirmed it. There was a high-end television and a few pop albums, but she didn't see a single book. A few glossy magazines were strewn on the nightstand.

She had always thought of her brother as a simple man, who tried to grab whatever he could from life without pondering any ethical implications. Come to think of it, she thought similarly of herself.

It was almost midnight. The list of things she'd need to take care of was almost finished. She had also called their aunt, who'd given her contact details for other relatives. The aunt had known about her brother's illness for a long time, and had therefore been expecting the news of his demise. She'd forgotten to ask her aunt how she had found out about her brother's illness.

She had been very nervous about having to explain over the phone that her brother had died. But in the end it came out as naturally as if she had been talking about some banal matter.

'He passed away last night... At the hospital... No, I wasn't with him, I didn't know that his condition was so serious... Yes, they should inform the closest relatives that a patient is dying... I won't file a complaint, there's no point.'

There's no *point*... There was no point explaining to her aunt that for months her brother hadn't been telling her the truth about his condition whenever they'd spoken on the phone.

She didn't understand why her brother had lied to her. Thankfully, there was a *universal* explanation: he didn't want to worry her, he didn't want her to keep visiting him and suffering. But she felt that there had to be some deeper meaning behind her brother's quasi-conspiratorial lies on the phone. At least if he had left a goodbye letter, she thought, but she immediately felt ashamed for even thinking that. Her brother's death wasn't a suicide; he died in a hospital after prolonged suffering. And when things got really bad, he couldn't write any more; just as the old nurse had said, he could barely hold a book during the last couple of weeks.

Once more her gaze landed on the book lying on the table. *New Mankind*, what a stupid title for a novel. It would have been much more fitting for a self-help book or a book on recent history. But the author must have known why he had chosen that title for his sci-fi novel.

She forced herself to continue reading. After a while she thought she had identified at least a minor *theme* in the story which could explain why her brother kept reading the book for months, over and over again. The novel's protagonist was a young man who was being stifled by a monotonous life in a small room of a cheap lodging house. Perhaps her brother was intrigued by the similarity—he too was confined to the small, utterly unpleasant space that was his hospital room. In a way, her brother was also unemployed, because he had nothing to do from morning until night, unless radiation therapy counted as some absurd type of activity.

The unemployed man from *New Mankind* was noticing *a transformation* taking place inside him. He was becoming more and more fatigued, sometimes he was in pain, but at the same time he felt that all of that would end soon, and he'd enter a new stage of life.

She didn't like books or movies that were about something fantastic or unrealistic. Reading *New Mankind* required a lot of effort on her part. The main idea of the novel— that in the bosom of contemporary mankind there grows a new biological breed, the future mankind—was repulsive to her. She wasn't *used to* such stories. To make matters worse, she didn't care for the author's writing style either. Long, complicated sentences, unclear transitions between dialogue and narrative intrusions, philosophy and values completely foreign to her.

Yet this book had captivated her brother so much during the final weeks of his life that he had been able to read a single page for hours on end. She wanted to know *why*. She had an inexplicable sense of guilt for not having spent time with her brother over the last few months, for underestimating his illness, and by reading this book she was paying a debt, overcoming a barrier that stood between her and her dead brother.

She felt that a similar *barrier* was being described in the book. The young man, who sensed that a person of the new mankind was growing inside him, gradually limited and broke off contact with other people. Relationships with things around him were a spider's web from which he had to free himself if he wanted *it* to keep maturing and growing inside him.

The new mankind wasn't just physically different, but also psychologically. The book's protagonist belonged to the chosen few who carried the future people inside them. His organs were undergoing mutations—they grew or shrank—and his relationship to the old mankind was also changing. His senses and perception were heightened. He could clearly see the mistakes people were making, and almost painfully sense all the imperfection and evil in his surroundings. That was why he isolated himself. He limited contact only to the most essential.

She thought the young man she was reading about was insane. And the book's author, Jerry Howland Jr., *must have been* half insane too.

It occurred to her that her brother's mind, exhausted by a long, untreatable illness, could have been—like the character in the book—sensitive to all the negative human character traits and actions in its surroundings. Perhaps his condition could have been called insanity. What if he didn't want to see her precisely because he was afraid that their in-person contact would harm him in some strange, paranoid way? Or, more accurately: this book had *put the idea into his head* that their meeting would harm him, which was why he lied to her on the telephone.

Her brother was living on the brink of death under tremendous psychological pressure, and this insane novel was the reason he had closed himself off further. Angry, she threw the book on to the table. She sprang up from the armchair. She took a shower. Despite the uncomfortable feeling she had when she was lying down in her brother's bed, she fell asleep almost instantly.

But she didn't sleep long. Distant noise woke her up. Milk delivery people were probably unloading crates in front of a shop. It was quarter past five. She got up and went to the kitchen to get a drink of water. Then she lay down again, even though she knew she wouldn't go back to sleep. She turned on the lamp. *Certain* that she wouldn't learn anything interesting, but curious to see how far the author was capable of taking his fantasies, she reached for *New Mankind.*

Her eyes burned, as they always did when she didn't get enough sleep. Yet she kept on reading, even though she held the book with aversion, as if it were the weapon that had killed her brother. The plot moved very slowly. Just like at the beginning. Inside the protagonist's body, a more perfect being kept developing. At the right time, for which the young man was getting ready, the new being was supposed to emerge from him like a butterfly from a chrysalis.

She noticed that Jerry Howland Jr. was succumbing to a certain pathetic, lofty style. He kept using more and more flowery metaphors, which didn't fit with the cold, dark tone he had adopted in the first half of the book. He wrote that the new people gifted with much more perfect abilities were discarding the remnants of their old bodies like skin they no longer needed, in order to step out, or more likely *take off*, towards a new life in a new world. This new world was described only hazily. It was some other dimension interconnected with three-dimensional space, but at the same time it exceeded it in a way that the old people couldn't understand or perceive.

'How pathetic. A shrivelled-up skin stays here, and the new man flies towards a space with different physical and chemical properties, which can only be perceived and taken advantage of by members of the new mankind.' She sighed and set the book aside in disgust.

This time she put down that idiotic novel for good, because it was almost eight o'clock. It was high time to *do things*. When she pictured the places and meetings that awaited her that day, fear and anxiety twisted her stomach into a knot. Pathology, funeral home, cemetery office, lawyer's office.

As soon as she got out of the elevator in the hospital basement, she received the first blow, which made it clear how difficult all the things she'd have to go through would be. A robust, dishevelled woman was gripping the handle of the door that said 'Pathology', crying desperately.

'Oh, my husband, what's left of you? You were so strong, and now all that's lying here is a pitiful skeleton with skin stretched over it. Where have all your strength and beauty gone? Why did you leave me in this evil world?'

She walked around the woman to get to the doorbell. In that split second an unclear memory of something from Jerry Howland Jr.'s novel flashed through her mind. But when her index finger touched the button, the unexpectedly loud and unpleasant buzz of the doorbell brought her back to *reality*.

Black & White

A black and white photograph is colour-blind. And its fate defies logic. Undoubtedly, it gives the photographer less creative space than a colour photograph, because it can only make use of white, black, and shades of grey. Grey itself could be considered a shade of black, since it's actually light black.

A black and white photograph does not depict the world in its true colours. It is less realistic and less authentic, it lags behind a colour photograph in its artistic possibilities as well as its documentary uses. And yet—while amateur photographers have been using colour film for years, professionals stick to monochrome. Nowadays you can only get black and white film in specialised shops. In no other medium do professionals use a developmentally lower level of technology than mass users. Only in photography.

I study the history and development of media. The exhibition *The Thirteenth Christmas* interested me not because of its topic (societal changes at home and in our neighbouring countries over the last twenty-five years following the fall of the dictatorships), but because of the technology it was using. I knew that the sole condition placed on the exhibiting photographers from all seven participating countries was to use only black and white photographs. I wanted to see how individual artists contended with the fact that they had to capture the pulsating—or more precisely, flashing—multi-coloured world of recent years in photos with no colour.

I expected the exhibition not to garner much public attention, but finding the exhibition hall completely empty was a shock. A retiree volunteer was sitting by the door, and her beige suit seemed like an out-of-place extravagance in the sea of black and white. The organiser had given her an important task—to force every visitor to sign his or her name at least once in a thick notebook immediately upon entry, which was supposed to document that this international exhibition enjoyed great popularity in our country.

I added my name to the column of about ten signatures under today's date. Relishing my own joke, I added the word 'fascinating' next to my signature, even though I had yet to see a single photograph.

I'm fascinated by the ability of a colour-blind lens to highlight whatever the photographer chooses. This exhibition was no different. One of the pictures had captured a forest of men's clenched fists at some protest, yet you couldn't miss a woman's slight fistlet, even though it was somewhere at the back. Right next to it was a stylised snapshot full of big, bright eyes of Roma children, yet the viewer's attention was drawn to the smallest girl with dishevelled hair, sitting on a short wall at the back with her eyes closed. She looked as though she was dreaming, which was why the photograph was entitled *Expectations*.

A monochromatic photo is the bearer of sad news. Even the elated crowds of black and white people from the first days of the revolution against the dictatorship looked as though, at the moment of their victory, they already carried within them the disillusionment of the years that would follow. Next there were the happy faces of the dissidents, whose fate after entering real politics was already inscribed on them: corrupt, incompetent, demagogic, or at least lonely.

I walked from one photograph to another. I didn't let myself be disturbed by a group of high-school girls who had entered the room briefly, perhaps only to turn around and slam the big door behind them, laughing.

Even though the authors of the pictures were agency, news, or art photographers from different countries of our region, the development looked the same everywhere. After the fall of a dictatorship, hurrying people with weary faces, arrogant nouveau riche, unscrupulous prostitutes, self--assured drug dealers, tattered beggars, and resigned old men appeared on the streets.

This is Bucharest? I asked myself when I read the title of the next photograph, because the same night-time scene could have been photographed in our country. This man lives in Krakow? I was surprised to see a person with large plastic bags and a familiar face in a different photograph. Another panel captured a family leaving a brightly lit supermarket with their Christmas shopping. When I read the description, I nodded happily. I had finally guessed correctly: those people really were from our country.

Next came the handing out of food to the poor on Christmas Eve at some train station, then a priest talking with two punk rockers, and in the back left corner there was a photograph which made me go weak at the knees. I had to hold on to one of the panels to keep my balance. It was...

She was in that photograph. Her eyes big and curious, her lips a little open and ready to enjoy a cigarette, as always. Her small nose, furrowed brow, pale cheeks, pointy chin. It was her.

Years ago I had taken all the photographs and videotapes of her to the basement, where they remained to this day. And now her eyes were looking at me curiously from a large photograph. And I was looking at them, confused.

I honestly felt more confusion than sadness. I turned around and quickly walked towards the door. I was running away from that photograph. I kept telling myself that I was just going out to get some fresh air. But I was running away like a coward.

I don't remember how I made it to the riverbank. I must have crossed a street and jumped over a fairly high stone wall. I have no idea how I did it, or why I went there. Perhaps I just needed to hide, to be alone in order to come to terms with my confusion.

The December air combined with river mist helped me recover. I took deep breaths of the cold air. It gave me strength. I knew that I'd go back to the exhibition that day. But first I needed to name and organise everything logically.

There was actually nothing unusual about it. Someone had simply taken a photo of her back then. By chance. It could have been five years ago, maybe seven. No, not seven. She was just an ordinary student back then. Uninteresting for the lens of a photographer working in black and white.

She didn't start with it until later, during the summer, six and a half years ago. I found out about it in the autumn, around October. We spent that Christmas together, but by the next one she was gone. Between the two was her springtime attempt at recovery. She had no help; I didn't interfere in her business. I didn't know how to protect her anyway. She lasted two months. That was what she told me; in reality, she may have only lasted two weeks. To this day I don't believe her…

I didn't notice whether the photograph was taken at Christmas, like the majority of the pictures in the exhibition.

If it was, it must have been six years ago, because they couldn't have photographed her any more at Christmas five years ago.

I walked back slowly. Even though an icy wind was blowing, and the previous night's frost was still hanging on in a few places, I could feel myself perspiring. I must have had wet spots under my arms, and I felt dampness around my collar. Over the years I had cried so many times, but this time I had yet to shed a single tear. It was too sudden; it called for a more extreme reaction than crying.

I entered the exhibition hall slowly, almost fearfully. I humbly fulfilled the request of the old lady by the entrance, and without unnecessary explanations I signed the guest book for the second time. Then I crossed out the word 'fascinating', which I had written half an hour earlier.

Slowly, I came up to the first panel of photographs, as if I didn't believe that I had already been there. All the images started to pass in front of my eyes anew. Clenched fists, eyes of Roma children, dance of the victorious revolution, exuberant dissidents. And again, the weary faces of everydayness, the arrogance of the nouveau riche, hookers, drug dealers, beggars' signs, and old men with their resignation. And one more time, snowy streets at night, branded bags in the hands of an old man, the shopping family, Christmas Eve dinner for the poor, priest and punk rockers… It was up next.

Undoubtedly, it was her. I only looked at her face for a brief moment, then I forced my eyes to pay attention to other aspects of the photograph. But they glanced at her again. I got them under control again, so that they'd go back to paying attention to the space and things around her.

I didn't recognise the evening street. In the distance there were headlights. I couldn't identify the brightly lit store-fronts; they were intentionally blurred. The photographer had wanted it that way; it wasn't because of the tears in my eyes, which had finally burst their banks.

Most likely she was sitting on a bench. She was wearing what she wore almost all the time during those months: a denim jacket with metal rivets on the collar, a thick pull-over sticking out from underneath it, a cashmere scarf, and wide trousers. Bracelets sparkled on her wrist. I stared at her face. The photographer had captured her as she was about to put a cigarette up to her mouth. Back then she had the habit of holding even regular cigarettes between her thumb and middle finger, as if they were marijuana.

Something kept bothering me. There was a newspaper spread across her lap, and it looked as though she had stopped reading it only to have her picture taken. But she hated newspapers. To her, they symbolised the world of well-informed careerists, and the saps who tried to emu-late them by at least reading the sports and crime sections.

Other people hate television for the same reason; for her, it was newspapers.

She had always had beautiful eyes. The first thing all that crap usually empties is a person's gaze, but her eyes remained big and curious. They were looking at me, as if they were asking whether I was still so sure that I had done everything I could to protect her back then.

It goes without saying that I had blamed myself a hundred times. I should have had more patience; I should have thrown my principles out the window. In some situations you should set aside your own ideals, forget societal conventions, and protect the person you love most. Had I had more love than principles five and a half years ago, we could have been standing next to each other now and looking at a photograph of some other girl bringing a cigarette up to her lips and reading a newspaper.

That newspaper… I was sure she hadn't read it. Maybe she had those things wrapped in it. Syringe, spoon, lighter, straw, or whatever it was she used. By then she looked down her nose at plain marijuana.

I tried to make out the title. A newspaper can also be identified by its typesetting or font. But when I looked more closely, I realised it was German. The word *Zeitung* was clear. Underneath it was the date. She knew the language well, and several German papers were sold in our country.

I looked at the numbers in the date over and over again. I kept tilting my head, coming closer, pulling back. It made no sense. The day this newspaper was printed was already three months after she had...

Three months before that newspaper was printed, policemen informed me how it had happened. They said that for some time she had been living with three junkies in an abandoned cottage. This was the second time they had started a fire. But this time they didn't manage to get out of there. Even paint thinner—their cheapest drug—fed the flames. All the bodies were burned beyond recognition. They didn't want to show them to me, and I didn't want to see them. They kept trying to persuade me not to insist on DNA identification. They said they'd have to send the sample—fire turns a person into a sample—abroad. I had no reason to ask for such a thing.

The photographer's name was listed as *Droxxi*. Did the pseudonym imply that the photographer was also connected to drugs? That actually didn't matter to me. All I wanted to know was when and where he had photographed her. I looked all over the snapshot again, but I found no other indication of the time and place.

I asked the old lady in beige at the entrance for a catalogue to get more information about *Droxxi*. She said they had run out. She wasn't even able to tell me where I could find the curator or organiser of the exhibition. All she gave me was a prepared, dubious-sounding excuse that he had gone to America, because there was a likelihood the exhibition would travel there.

I walked through the exhibition hall towards the photograph again, but shortly afterwards the woman by the entrance asked me to leave, because they were closing at four that day.

At home I immediately started to search the Internet for *Droxxi*. The first *Droxxi* was an overconfident Norwegian high-school student, who on his website called himself a singer, composer, lyricist, and performer. From his short bio I figured out that at the time the photograph had been taken, he was nine years old. The second *Droxxi* was an international distributor of cosmetics, drugstore merchandise, and pharmaceuticals. The third *Droxxi*, which was short for Doctor OxyGenius X, was a home air purifier for people with allergies. I kept looking through other pages. Sex, sci-fi, baseball, and all kinds of other *Droxxi*.

Finally I ran across something on a university website. 'The work of the Hungarian photographer Robi Rónay draws on the philosophy of naturalistic portraiture developed by the legendary *Droxxi* group.' Nothing more.

That night I couldn't have cared less about the things I was supposed to do. I didn't take *her* dog for a walk. I didn't go and air out the basement. I kept flying tirelessly through the infinite spaces of the Internet. I pictured having *Droxxi*, most likely a bohemian with injection bruises on his fore-arm, in a chokehold and beating him until he recalled when and where he had taken that photograph.

I fell asleep with my head on the keyboard. In the wee hours of the morning I stretched out on the living-room couch. I couldn't wait to go back to the exhibition. First and foremost, I had to get in touch with the organisers. They could tell me who *Droxxi* was—or were.

I don't know why, but in the morning I changed my mind. I went to the university library and then to the city gallery. I looked for any mention of the *Droxxi* group. The more magazines and books I searched, the more energy I had for looking at others. But I wasn't finding anything. I stopped my useless search around noon so that I could finally go to the exhibition. It was another unpleasant, chilly day.

The same old lady stood in the doorway of the exhibition hall. She was wearing her beige suit. At first she didn't want to let me in, because the exhibition *The Thirteenth Christmas* had supposedly been cancelled. I skipped the pleasantries and pushed my way in.

She had been telling the truth. Half the panels were gone. The last one, which no longer had a photo on it, was the one I had come to see. The old woman was mad at me and didn't want to tell me anything. She just kept berating me for shoving my way in so rudely.

Shortly, two men in overalls came in and started to take down the remaining panels. They packed the photographs into wooden crates. Begrudgingly they told me that the first half of the photos had left on a truck about an hour ago. They didn't know where it was going. Then the woman in beige approached us. With a smirk she said that the truck was headed for Germany, and from there the photos would fly to America. She added spitefully that she remembered very well how I didn't believe her the other day when she told me about the curator's trip to America. Indeed, things had worked out: the exhibition was on its way there.

I went back home. I finally took the dog for a walk. I tried to suppress my emotions and rationally consider my next steps. *Droxxi* had vanished like a mirage. I had to determine the day and location of the photo shoot some other way.

Around five, I started to make dinner. I heated up a can in a small pot and poured the rest of yesterday's tea into a plastic cup. Then I picked it all up and went down to the basement. As soon as I opened the door, I heard the rustling of steps and the rattling of a chain. She hadn't eaten anything since the previous morning. But I decided I wouldn't give her any food or drink until she told me the truth. I had to know how she had got out that day five years ago, and why some asshole had taken a photo of her. If I didn't find out, I couldn't be sure that I'd really be able to protect her now.

Visiting Mother

He awoke from a short, unsettling dream in which Marta was walking up a set of stairs towards him. Their surroundings were indistinct and immersed in a white glow; it was impossible to tell whether they were indoors or outdoors. In his dream he was standing on an upper landing, waiting for Marta to come to him. He wanted to go on, but she kept calling for him to wait. She wasn't far, but the number of steps kept growing, so she wasn't getting any closer.

He stayed in bed a little longer. His dream had left him with an unpleasant sense of incompleteness, of unfulfilled desire. It occurred to him that he should take a greater—and more active—interest in when Marta would be released from the hospital. Perhaps he should insist on her release, since her condition had improved significantly.

When it comes to hallucinations and illusions, it's often impossible to determine a clear diagnosis. It's just a battle for a change of reality. A physician can say that a patient has an ulcer, which is then surgically removed, but psychological disorders are not measurable, which means that their improvement is also not measurable. And Marta had been presenting much better over the past few weeks. Actually, she was just like before, normal. He decided he'd ask for her to be released without further ado. It seemed that for several days even the chief physician had been hesitant to offer an opinion on Marta's condition.

He got up and got dressed. For years Marta had been the one taking care of him. He had got used to her making him breakfast while he saw to his morning hygiene. They ate breakfast together, and as he was finishing, Marta went to set out a shirt and suit for him for work. When their daughter, Ema, was still little, Marta got her impeccably dressed too. Then he drove their daughter to school. When Ema turned fifteen, she started to attend a music conservatory in the next town. She only came home on the weekends.

In the years that followed, Marta turned her full attention on him. It was necessary, because in his position a wrinkled suit could have signalled a lack of seriousness, and a lack of seriousness could have turned into multi-million losses for the firm. Marta became his professional image-maker. She kept abreast of magazines, selected his outfits based on them, and made decisions about which social events he should attend.

Now he had to do it all himself. He had no trouble making coffee and pouring yoghurt over his cereal; the trouble was life without Marta. He loved her, which meant that he had got used to her and needed to have her close by.

When he started the car, he glanced at the dashboard. It was five to eight. He was going to be late again. For years he had demanded that his subordinates be on time; the operational meeting had to start at quarter past eight even if a foot of snow had fallen. Over the last few months, the meeting had regularly got pushed to eight-thirty. He realised that it would also be better for the firm if Marta came home.

While he was giving the secretary instructions, he noticed her cleavage. But his attention wasn't drawn to her rounded female curves, it was drawn to her neckline. Was it just his imagination, or had the young woman really begun to dress in a more revealing manner over the past few weeks? He closed the door to his office behind her and tried to remember whether she had worn such short skirts and tight blouses before. Perhaps she thought that now that his wife was in the hospital, there was a chance... He didn't feel like fleshing out his suspicion, but in his mind he put a question mark by the secretary. If he noticed any other similar indications, he'd replace her.

The meeting went as usual. The department heads wanted to make their departments' work easier, so they kept suggesting that part of their workload be moved to others. He let them argue a little and throw blame around. Then he decided that everything would remain as it was, but there would be more stringent quality control. The result was that the different departments would have to keep an eye on each other.

The meeting ended. He looked at the backs of his departing colleagues. None of them had become his friends. They were just overeager subordinates. He could trust them to fulfil his orders, but he couldn't confide in them. Perhaps if he had a friend there, he'd have an easier time living without Marta. Luckily, he didn't have a friend, and he was missing his wife more and more, so he was going to do everything he could to get her home. Not only because he wanted to have her by his side, but also because it was becoming more and more obvious to him that Marta was fine.

He called the hospital. He wanted to set up a meeting with the chief physician, but a woman's voice told him that the chief physician was on holiday all week. He decided to go to see Marta's attending physician that day or the next. He was going to ask him about the prognosis of Marta's illness, and perhaps check out some books on the subject as well. Then, when he went to see the chief physician the following week, he'd already know something about the diagnosis and be able to present an argument.

He ate lunch at a restaurant that had become his favourite over the last few weeks. When Marta was hospitalised, he started to look for a place that offered honest-to-goodness home cooking. He and Marta often went out to dinner, but on those occasions they sought out the exact opposite—something exotic, like Mexican, Thai, or Arab cuisine. But now he wanted meals that most closely resembled Marta's cooking. Without processed-food side dishes or instant soups, without tinned mushrooms or vegetables.

He ended up finding a small restaurant on a side street, which had awful decor. The walls were covered in artwork from the last century, the tables and chairs were made to resemble a rustic style, but the tablecloths had pop art motifs. Marta would have said that it looked terrible—and she would have been right. She may even have suggested that a person in his position and with his level of responsibility for the firm should not go to such restaurants. But he would have assuaged her with a caress and a smile.

Marta was attentive, to the point of being a perfectionist. Perhaps this fixation had contributed to the decline of her mental health. She lived in constant stress because she felt responsible for him. In the future, he'd try to temper that; they'd focus on more important things. They couldn't be nothing more than representatives of the firm from morning till night. Once in a while they had to be ordinary spouses who loved each other, even in public.

Other people experienced a lull after lunch. But he always found coffee to be a sufficient pick-me-up. He buried himself in work. After an hour he realised that he hadn't been thinking about Marta at all, and he felt guilty. It made him so distracted that he had no more energy for work. Separation from Marta and her—for the first time he referred to it as 'incarceration'—at the clinic were taking a toll on his life, too. If it didn't end soon, he'd have to go to see a psychologist. He smiled at the thought of the most modern romantic story about faithful married love: in order for the loving husband to be with his wife, he has to be hospitalised with her at the psychiatric clinic. But that wasn't going to happen. He'd get Marta out of the hospital, even if he had to sign a waiver. If necessary, he'd get a second opinion. But that might not be necessary; Marta really did appear very balanced.

Before leaving the office, he tried to call their daughter. She was also having a hard time with her mother's hospitalisation. She was coming home a lot less than she used to.

Maybe she hadn't even told her friends. At the age of twenty, there's no greater humiliation than having your mother on a psychiatric ward. He got her voicemail. Ema must have been in class.

On his way to the clinic, he stopped by the store. Marta was not happy with the hospital food. She complained about not getting enough fruit. So he always brought her some. Today he spotted small containers of blueberries on the shelf. Given the season, Marta was going to be surprised.

It was the afternoon rush hour. His car inched towards the suburb where the clinic was located. He wondered whether he should tell Marta that he was going to fight for her release. It might be better to wait until he'd spoken with the chief physician next week. He didn't want to get her hopes up or to make explicit promises. He knew that Marta wanted to go home, and that was the important thing. But what if the chief physician insisted on more tests?

He parked on the small paved area in front of the clinic. When he got out of the car, he looked up at Marta's window. He had got there a little earlier than usual, so she wasn't waiting for him yet. The main entrance was unlocked, and the front desk was empty. He didn't run into anyone upstairs either. Even the entrance to the ward was open. As his hand touched the doorknob of Marta's room, it occurred to him that he could take her away from there, and no one would stop them.

When he appeared at the door, Marta jumped up from an armchair and embraced him. Their kiss lasted longer than usual. In his lower abdomen he felt that his body also wanted Marta to come home. He asked her what was new. She said that the boredom had reached a new high, and was approaching its limit. She quipped that she'd certainly not be the first person to go insane on a psychiatric ward. He nodded, pleased, because her answers confirmed that Marta was fully recovered.

Marta had the most expensive room in the whole clinic. It was a private room with a good view, as well as its own toilet and shower. While he was washing the blueberries for her in the bathroom, someone knocked on the door.

'Hi, Mum,' Ema said hesitantly.

'Ema, I'm so glad to see you,' Marta said cheerfully. Then she added: 'Come on in and close the door.'

'How are you doing, Mum? You look very happy today.'

'I'm glad we're together again.'

'Me too.'

'Dad's in the bathroom, washing the blueberries he brought me. You'll have some, won't you?'

'What blueberries, Mum? What are you talking about again? Stop imagining Dad. Stop making up his life; he's been dead for six months now. When will you come to terms with that?'

Story with a Florist

I was supposed to meet a certain young woman that day, whose ad in the personals I had answered. As I was passing by a small florist's shop in one of the side streets a few minutes before our agreed-upon meeting time, I realised that I had forgotten to get flowers.

I went into the tiny shop with the intention of buying a small bouquet. One that wouldn't get in the way, and moreover, one that would last without water through the theatre performance to which I was about to take the woman from the ad. I said something to that effect to the woman behind the counter (without mentioning the ad, of course).

'I'm sorry, I can't help you. I don't sell cut flowers, only potted plants,' she said brusquely.

I looked at her, taken aback. In the past I had only bought flowers on rare occasions, and I had no idea that there were florist's shops which didn't sell cut flowers.

'So you can't make me a bouquet?' I asked.

'A traditional one? An ordinary bouquet? No. But I can offer you several flowering plants in pots. They won't just last through the whole performance, but much, much longer,' the florist said with a smile.

She pointed to a shelf. The selection was impressive. There were blue flowers on short stems, tall plants with red petals, majestic white compound flowers resembling tiny balloons. Other flowers were yellow, purple, or orange. But the one that caught my eye had lovely pink flowers and variegated leaves with clearly delineated light and dark green areas.

'I'd like that plant, please.' I pointed. 'The one with spots on the leaves.'

The saleswoman nodded, as if she were pleased with my choice. She carefully picked up the pot and set it in front of me. She said two Latin words, which must have been the name of the plant.

'Beautiful, isn't it?' She sighed. There was almost a parental pride in her voice.

I watched the saleswoman's fingers as they skilfully wrapped the plant in decorative paper. Then I looked up at her face. I wished that the woman I was about to meet would be as beautiful as this nature lover.

Before I paid, she gave me a long list of instructions on how to take care of the plant. It should be placed where it wasn't draughty. But not in the kitchen, because the steam could harm it. It needed to be watered daily, but in small amounts. Whenever I added more soil, it had to be alkaline.

'And go easy on the fertiliser,' she said in closing.

'There's so much to remember that I'll have to come back tomorrow and write it down,' I said. I wanted it to come off as a joke. At the same time, I was so taken with her uninhibited love of nature that I was completely serious.

As I was leaving the shop, I looked at my watch. I should have been at the fountain, the place I had suggested for the meeting, five minutes ago. It took me a little longer to get there.

The whole way I kept coming up with excuses. Showing up ten minutes late to a first date calls for an impeccable excuse. I ended up deciding to tell the truth. I was late because I was buying the plant, and the saleswoman gave me excessively detailed care instructions.

In the end I didn't have to apologise at all. The woman who had posted the ad was no longer at the fountain. I took a good look around, but I didn't see a woman in a brown suit holding a newspaper (those were the identifying marks we had agreed on).

I felt relieved. The florist had captivated me so much that any other woman would have been lacklustre and boring by comparison. I wandered around. Memories of the fingers wrapping the pot surfaced in my mind, of the pale yet beautiful lips explaining how to water the plant.

I made a quick decision that was completely out of character for me. I decided to go back to the flower shop and try to introduce myself to the saleswoman.

By the time I arrived at the shop, it was already closed. Through the glass door, I could see the young florist carrying some of the pots to the back of the store.

I knocked. She came to the door and looked at me through the glass. Then she unlocked the door and pushed it open a crack. We looked at each other. All of a sudden I didn't know what to say.

'I'd like to return this,' I blurted out and shoved the wrapped pot into her hands.

She didn't say anything. She was waiting for me to say something more.

'I hope you'll understand,' I said, looking for the right words. 'The beauty of this flower deserves the best care. And only you can provide that.'

She whispered something along the lines that I was right, and thanked me for recognising that. Before locking the door, she said I could come back sometime and see how my plant was doing.

The next day I started thinking about the florist first thing in the morning. I couldn't concentrate on my work and was distracted. I went to the shop around the same time as the previous day. She was helping an older woman. She greeted me, but she didn't seem surprised. I waited while she explained to the customer how to take care of the cowslips she was buying.

'Did you come to see your beauty?' she asked me with a smile when we were alone.

'Yes,' I said, caught off guard by her self-confidence. It took me a few seconds to realise that she hadn't used the word beauty to refer to herself, but to the plant I had bought.

She told me that the plant was in the back room. She hadn't left it in the front so that she wouldn't have to explain over and over again that it wasn't for sale.

'Would you keep an eye on the shop?' she asked. 'I'll bring it right out.'

A moment later I was looking at the large flowers of 'my'

plant. It had nice pink blossoms, but it wasn't until then that I got a closer look at the bizarre colour of its leaves. I thought that the light and dark areas resembled the backs of frogs or lizards. The leaves were hanging down, as if they were tired. I asked the florist whether the leaves shouldn't be more upright. She explained to me in detail that during the day the leaves stretched out towards the sun, but in the evening they drooped, resting. She suggested that one day I should come over around noon.

'You'd be surprised by the very different charm of this plant at that hour. Right now it's a tired club dancer, but during the day she looks like a ballerina in a solo performance,' she said.

Naturally, the next day I used my lunch break to come and see my ballerina.

'If you were to cut it, it would wilt in two to three hours. That's why I couldn't sell cut flowers. They're basically fresh corpses,' the young florist said. I thought that her words were not only logical, but also carried an ecological or moral message.

'This way I get to see my plant again tomorrow. And when these flowers wither, at some point there'll be new ones, right? I'll come to see those too,' I said, and my own words filled me with hope.

I came over almost every day. I was completely smitten with the florist. Her fingers amid the vines and leaves; her smile, which she bestowed upon me more and more often;

her eyes of an indescribable colour, as if they had absorbed the glow of all the plants they looked at.

Her name was Valentina. I devoured every word she uttered. I was learning how to take care of different plants. I was figuring out what type of soil they needed, how to water them, in which months they bloomed. Although I still had trouble putting the right name with each plant, because many of the names sounded alike, I was becoming an expert on flora. My prior knowledge was limited to the fact that geraniums smelled bad. But now I knew, among other things, that the plant with a lot of red flowers was called *Rhododendron Baden-Baden*. I was no longer mistaking the pinkish-yellow flowers of *Clematis montana* for strawberries, and I was able to identify the miracle worker of the genus *Mimulus*. I even managed to make myself useful and separate clumps of cowslips when it was time to repot them.

I was in love with the florist, and by being with her, I was developing a passion for the green world around her.

Sometimes I came to see Valentina at lunch, other times I stopped by on my way back from work. And when I had business to take care of at a nearby office, I took the opportunity to visit her during working hours. After about two or three weeks, I was almost certain that Valentina didn't have a boyfriend. I had spent many hours in her shop at different times of day, but no one she knew had ever come by.

For the time being, we were just friends. I really enjoyed listening to her talk about her plants. I liked to ask her where they were from. Then we usually tried to picture what might be happening around the plant if it were in its natural habitat. We imagined large venomous spiders, shrieking parrots, mischievous monkeys, or motionless snakes lying in wait.

Whenever I was at the flower shop in the evening, I helped Valentina carry the potted plants that had to be in the back for the night. I was only allowed to go into the first room. It was long and narrow. A glass ceiling allowed it to serve as a greenhouse. Valentina explained that she mostly grew shade-loving plants, which didn't mind less light.

The second room contained something that my beautiful florist called the secret of her success as a grower.

One night after about a month I walked her home for the first time. She lived close by, in an old, hardly maintained apartment building. She pointed out the two small windows of her apartment. It was an unpleasant surprise to see the poor conditions in which Valentina was living. Even though I didn't go in, I had no doubt that her furnishings would have been quite modest.

On my way home, I tried to make sense of it. I saw the beautiful florist in a whole new light. I finally gave an appropriate label to her simple style of dress—poor. It became clear why she was evasive whenever I asked her about her favourite holiday spots or restaurants she liked. She couldn't afford any of those things. I knew that she owned her shop, but I hadn't realised that her business generated minimal profit. It should have been obvious from the get-go. Too few people visited a florist's shop on a tucked-away street, and Valentina's merchandise was too specialised.

I wondered how I could help her. She was happy among her flowers, so that certainly could not change. But she should be thinking about her own well-being more than about the living conditions of her plants.

When I came to Valentina's shop the next day, it was already closing time. I intended to speak with her alone. I wanted to hint to the florist that her future could also be my future.

First, she showed me a camellia. She pointed out the unusual sheen of its evergreen leaves.

'The sheen reminds me of tears,' she said.

'But the flowers suggest that they are tears of happiness,' I said.

'This plant blooms for several weeks, but its leaves look like this all year,' Valentina said, and started in on her regular evening tasks.

As we were carrying the plants into the back, I asked her how much money she had made that day. She didn't respond immediately, but gave me a look of surprise, or perhaps even distrust.

'I sold about as much as usual,' she said noncommittally.

'Little, then,' I said harshly and grabbed her hands.

She gently freed herself and picked up another flowerpot. But I took it from her and set it on the counter.

'Valentina, I really care about you. Please, hear me out. Yesterday I saw where you live, and I realised that you're very poor. I want to help you.'

'I don't need anyone's help,' she shouted, and ran into the next room.

I followed her, and without saying another word I helped her water the plants.

When we were done with the work, she let herself be persuaded to hear me out. Slowly, I explained that her shop was in a terrible location. It was never going to make her a fortune. She was angry, and I knew that she wanted to say that she was happy even without money. But I didn't let her interrupt. I told her that I could see how happy she was surrounded by flowers, and that was the direction in which she should plan her future. Of course, she had no idea where I was headed with that, but it looked as though she was starting to listen to me with more and more interest.

'Valentina, I think you like growing flowers more than you like selling them. Am I right?' I asked.

She agreed.

'I'm offering you a partnership. You'll reduce your opening hours a little in order to be able to spend more time propagating plants. The first of the back rooms, the one you let me into, is half empty anyway. Over time you'll fill it with plants, which you won't just sell in this shop, but can offer to other flower shops as well. I propose a partnership. I'll be your business representative, negotiating sales with the other shops. At first I'll keep my current job and do this on the side, but once the business starts doing well, I'll sell flowers full-time,' I said. I'm sure the excited expression on my face revealed even the things I didn't have the courage to say.

Valentina was silent for a long time. Then she quietly asked:

'Are you really serious?'

'Yes,' I said.

'Then come with me! I'll show you my secret… The secret of my business…' she said. She took me by the hand and dragged me behind her to the back of the building, which she had never wanted to show me before.

It looked almost the same as the first room, except that there was a lot less space. The other difference was that the plants were potted in soil in aquaria or in large glass preserving jars. Valentina bent down and handed me a jar. It was an *Anemone nemorosa* with pinkish flowers. A particularly nice specimen. I took the plant and praised its shape. And I awaited the revelation of Valentina's big secret.

'Take a good look at it,' she said solemnly.

I kept turning the preserving jar in my hands in order to see this rhizomatous plant from every angle. But there was nothing on it.

'Look lower,' Valentina said. I looked at the bottom of the jar. In a few places I saw the hair-like root ends, but I couldn't tell what made them special.

'I think something's moving in there,' I finally said.

'You got it! It's an earthworm. Each of these jars contains one or two earthworms. They are quite beneficial for the plants. They aerate the soil and provide an ideal fertiliser—vermicompost. I've not heard of anyone else using them. But I am convinced they'll bring me great success as a grower,' Valentina said with pride.

I must have looked disappointed, because she quickly went on with her explanation.

'They're not local earthworms, but a rare South American variety. Some of the varieties from over there can get as long as six feet, but these are only a couple of inches long. They get sold here in pet shops as food for larger predatory fish. I bought them because I liked them. I saved them from being eaten by fish, and they're repaying me by helping my plants. I've had them for about two years. I don't even know which generation they are any more.'

She was very excited as she explained how she fed the earthworms straw, vegetable scraps, and rotten fruit. She showed me how she had to water their soil and direct light at them. But then she got quiet, as if she had revealed more than she had intended to. Not long after that she was dragging me out of there by my sleeve.

When we were back at the front of the shop, I didn't know what to say. Her secret seemed quite banal. I'd found out how naive Valentina was, yet I loved her all the more. I needed to file the earthworms in my mind, so as to assign them the appropriate importance. After all, they could have been critical and had the potential to bring us exceptional business success.

When I was saying goodbye to her that evening, I was taken aback by her request that in the future I should not enter the room containing the earthworms without her consent. She said she had entrusted me with her secret, and I had to respect her wishes.

Our relationship continued at its calm pace. I came to see Valentina every day, and we admired the beauty of plants together. But now we were also planning our joint enterprise. I made a list of nearby flower shops. When I walked Valentina home, we chose routes that allowed us to look at them one by one. Some of the shops seemed more focused on toys and souvenirs, others sold only cut flowers. But there were still plenty of potential customers.

I wanted to surprise Valentina for her birthday with the news that I had secured our first client to buy her plants. I started to look for an appropriate flower shop and prepared the necessary paperwork. Sales invoices and delivery slips are often more important than the actual merchandise.

I had no success in the first shop. The manager turned down some of the plants I was offering because he had never heard of anyone growing them in planters. According to him, they were plants suitable for a garden, and they couldn't thrive in an apartment. I explained to him that 'our company' had been growing them in planters for years, but he looked at me with distrust. When I was walking out of that flower shop, the thought crossed my mind that there really could be something to Valentina's earthworms. Perhaps it was thanks to them, or thanks to their organic castings, that she was able to grow plants that others couldn't.

Unfortunately, I had to stop my preparations for Valentina's birthday. My company sent me on a week-long business trip to Bulgaria, and I was supposed to get back on her birthday.

On the business trip, I fulfilled my duties with disinterest. I was on autopilot as I visited my assigned partners and informed them about our company's new regulations for foreign transactions, which had arisen from the last shareholder meeting. I no longer saw my future connected with this company; therefore, I limited my activities to the indispensable. I did my job, and nothing more. I spent my afternoons in flower shops. For hours I browsed the plants that were on offer. I was comparing them to Valentina's merchandise and looking for opportunities to use some of the things I was seeing in Bulgaria. I bought several dozen seed packets.

In a small shop near the hotel where I was staying, I found a beautiful *Scilla non-scripta* plant with elegant clusters of dark-blue flowers. I had never seen a flower of that colour before. Naturally, it was in a pot. Although the plant was very expensive, I had to buy it. It was the most beautiful present I could give Valentina. I was a little afraid of taking a planter on the airplane, but it turned out fine.

I rushed home from the airport to put away the plant. Then I called a cab and dashed to Valentina's shop. She was very glad to see me. I felt really bad lying to her that I had come straight from the airport. But I only said it to be able to make her birthday present perfect. I waited for a customer to walk into the shop and then whispered to her that I had to go to the bathroom.

The bathroom was at the end of the first of the two back rooms. Walking between the flowerpots made me realise how near and dear to my heart those plants had become in the time since I had met Valentina less than a year ago. There was the beautiful exotic redness that *Paeonia officinalis* exudes; a couple of feet over, pansies of every possible colour—burgundy and black, yellow and purple, pink and brown.

When I reached the back of the room, I turned around to make sure that Valentina couldn't see me. Then I quickly opened the door and slipped in to where the plants enriched by earthworm activity were. I kept picking up jars, looking for one in which I could see an earthworm through the glass, so that I wouldn't have to search for one in the dirt. I pulled out a spoon and a plastic bag from my pocket. I quickly dug out an earthworm and stuck it into the bag.

'I must go to the office now, but I'll be back this evening for sure, please wait for me,' I yelled to Valentina as I was leaving, likely confusing her by being in such a hurry.

I ran home as fast as I could. I repotted the Bulgarian plant into a small aquarium. In the rush I forgot the most important thing—I didn't place the earthworm into the soil. I didn't remember it until I was walking out, and I had to go back to dig it in.

By the time I made it to the flower shop, it was closed. I was standing there with a plant wrapped in decorative paper, knocking on the glass insert of the door, just like the day we met. Valentina saw me and smiled. As she opened the door, she was surprised to see what I was holding.

Of course she knew it was a plant, but she must not have realised that it was for her.

I wished her a happy birthday as I was walking in. I had planned what to say on the airplane, but in the moment I got completely mixed up.

'Valentina, I'm glad that I walked into this shop several months ago. I'm grateful that you taught me not only to understand flowers, but also to love them. I wish you a very happy birthday, and I hope we'll have many other occasions to celebrate together. The two of us,' I said. As I was saying the words, I knew they made no sense. What did it mean that I wanted us to have many other occasions to celebrate together? Utter nonsense. It was embarrassing.

I felt my ears blush. They must have turned red, just like when I was a kid embarrassed about something.

Valentina took the package I handed her. Patiently, without tearing the paper, she unwrapped it. She looked at the flower, and a happy smile spread across her face.

'It's beautiful, it's the most beautiful *Scilla non-scripta* I've ever seen. Thank you… And I hope we'll grow even more beautiful ones together,' she said, and with the flower in her hands she came up to kiss me. My gift was an obstacle between us, but our lips did meet.

I grabbed Valentina by the shoulders, but I didn't embrace her yet. I gently pushed her away from me.

'Valentina, you didn't take a good look at my present. Look again.'

She lifted up the plant and kept looking it over, smiling. Then she must have understood. She pursed her lips and stared at the glass aquarium in which the flower was planted. She turned it slowly until she spotted part of an earthworm.

She screamed, as if she were in great pain. She slammed the container on to the counter. With one swift motion she ripped out the plant, roots and all, and threw it on the ground. Her fingers started to dig in the soil that was left in the aquarium. Then she carefully grabbed the earthworm and took it out. She placed it in her hand and studied its undulating body.

'Oh, Albert, my Albert, what happened to you, you're covered in bruises. What awful wounds.' She spoke to the worm that was slowly twisting in her fingers. Then she stuck out her tongue and gently licked the slimy body.

Finally she turned towards me and yelled:

'You inconsiderate asshole, what have you done to my Albert? I wish you were dead!'

Somewhere on the Surface Is an Imperial Palace with Towers Whose Gilded Cupolas Gleam in the Midday Sun

> The priests led a prayer to Yahweh; they gave
> thanks that they were permitted to see so much and
> begged forgiveness for their desire to see more.
> Ted Chiang, 'Tower of Babylon'

Were I to say that the grandiose idea to dig to the bottom of the earth had been born in the exalted head of the great-grandfather of our current exalted emperor, I could be wrong. The truth is, I don't know who our emperor is at present. It has been years since anyone living on the surface has come down to us, the men opening the way to the bottom of the earth. I can make that claim despite the fact that I don't know the meaning of the word year, because I know that no one has brought us the latest news for a very, very long time. Everything we know has reached us third- or fourth-hand. It is possible that our country is now ruled by the son or the grandson of the emperor we still think sits on the throne and to whom we pay homage.

The caravans that deliver our supplies of food and drinking water from the earth's surface never come all the way to us. They stop after a few days' journey beneath the surface, and hand off their load to other bearers, who then carry it for several days until they reach the next station, where another group picks up the barrels and bags.

It has been said that the temperature, pressure, and fumes down here would kill the people who live on the earth's surface. Perhaps it's just a myth the commanders use to boost our morale. They often tell us that the people up above consider us heroes. Supposedly, even the exalted emperors themselves often speak about us, and priests regularly say prayers for us.

The temperature, pressure, and air quality don't bother us at all. We're used to them. Perhaps the air and light on the surface would kill us. Sometimes I wish I could see how the people up above live, but other times I worry that our job will be done one day, and we'll have to go up to the surface and be disappointed.

All of us down here are the children of diggers. Our fathers were also the children of diggers. Just like our parents, we don't know the exact meaning of words such as light, forest, or flower. Gradually we've stopped using them. Most of the time we talk about the rock we dig. Sturdy, cohesive, hard, resistant, fissile, crumbly, brittle, fragile, soft, rough, smooth, veiny, fissured, flaky, crystalline, grainy, streaked, damp, oily, delicate, heavy, light, transparent, translucent, clear, lustrous, opaque, dark, pale—those are the most important words in the language of the people down here.

On the surface lies our empire. They say it's not large, but it is quite wealthy, because it sells the iron ore and precious stones we mine down here to neighbouring countries. The people up there supposedly live in cities. The largest of them is the capital, where the exalted emperor and his dignitaries live. The imperial palace has many towers with gilded cupolas. It has been said that they gleam in the midday sun. We cannot imagine what those towers look like or how they gleam, because we have never seen the midday sun, although we can still remember our ancestors saying that the sun was above, in the sky. It has been said that there's only one sun, and it divides time into day and night. All we can see above are stars, and we use torches to have light while we work. Maybe the stories about the sun are just myths or fairy tales.

We have our own myths down here. When some of the men grumble about the exhausting work, they spread myths about how people up there no longer have to toil the way we do down here, because scholars have invented and constructed connected gears, belts, hooks, pickaxes, and shovels to do the work for them. But if we're really as important to the exalted emperors and the empire as our commanders lead us to believe, then such wonders would have to be working first and foremost down here.

Another myth says that the man who sees a living being on a rock he's dug up will soon die. I don't know of any-one who has seen such a thing, but I do know many who have died. Death comes after life. The only living beings I've ever seen other than people are donkeys. They haul up the rocks we've dug out. But even the donkeys we know have never been all the way up to the surface. After a few days' journey, they set down their load and come back. The broken rock is then loaded on to other animals called camels or horses, and they carry it up higher. The man who usually digs next to me has seen a horse. It is a four-legged animal similar to a donkey, but bigger. The salted meat we eat supposedly also used to be living beings, but we can't imagine what kind.

We spend a lot of time thinking and talking about what awaits us beneath the rock we're digging. Some think there's a large quantity of water there. If we open a path for it, it'll drown us all. I don't think that's possible, though. Water never comes in large quantities. There's little of it, and we must conserve it, because if a supply caravan is delayed, water becomes the most valuable commodity. The person who doesn't drink for a long time dies. I've known many people like that. Someone stole their water supplies, and if their commander or companions didn't help them, they died of thirst.

Others say that beneath the rock we keep digging there is another rock, and then another, and another. They say the rocks are endless. That sounds more plausible to me, since we've not encountered anything other than rocks so far. If the rock really is endless, we'll never find out.

The great emperor who had ordered the opening of a path to the bottom of the earth probably also didn't know what would be there. And the emperors who succeeded him on the throne didn't know either, and neither did their scholars nor the students of those scholars. The answer to this question is not in the libraries or archives of the emperor's palace, which has many towers with gilded cupolas gleaming in the midday sun. The answer is down here. That is the main purpose of our work. We, or our descendants, should one day discover what is at the very bottom of the earth. Then we will find out what the earth stands on and what is beneath it.

Lately, it seems that it's been getting warmer and warmer. Rumour has it that on the surface of the earth, warm and cold seasons alternate. Down here we've not had that so far, but it's possible that from some depth on, warm and cold seasons will also start alternating. Right now we're in a warm season, though I'd prefer a cold one, because the heat causes sweating, which increases water consumption. The commanders have already requested increased rations. But it will take a very long time for this request to reach the dignitaries on the surface who are qualified to evaluate it and make a decision. Even after the highest commanders approve it, many days will pass before the additional barrels of water and wine begin to reach us.

Because of the great heat, we now work naked. Our bodies are damp from perspiration. They glisten in the light of the torches like the hardest, heaviest rocks that we run across from time to time. One of the men, whose job it is to lift the rocks we break with our pickaxes, shrieked in pain. A boulder he touched had burned him. Indeed, when we touched the boulder with our fingers, it was hot.

We can feel the heat through our shoes. Every now and then, we sit on cooler boulders and lift our feet, because the heat from below is unbearable. The commanders are more confused than we are. From the moment they were placed in their positions, their only job was to make sure that we kept working. They know how to yell at us and whip us, but they don't understand what's happening. They've been huddling together and trying to decide what to do. We watch them in silence. The donkeys bray restlessly. They also feel the rising heat.

No one's working any more. We thought we'd wait for the rock to cool down a bit, but it's still just as hot.

Finally, one of the commanders couldn't take it any more. He used his whip to force his men to continue digging. They got up begrudgingly. Slowly, they started to chip at the rock with their pickaxes. When one of them pulled away a larger rock, he jumped aside, frightened. Out of the hole he had created shot a beam of white light. No torch is that bright.

The man covered his eyes and wailed. The rest of us cautiously approached the hole and the light. It burned our eyes even when we shaded them with our hands.

Gradually, we're getting used to the brightness. Even at the cost of damaging their vision, the most curious lean over the crack from which the bright light is emanating.

We're looking down into the hole. It seems that somewhere deep, deep beneath us there is a land, in the land a city, and in the city a palace, which has many towers with gilded cupolas. They gleam in the midday sun.

Abchan and Nasan

> For us the meaning of taboo branches off into two
> opposite directions. On the one hand it means to us
> sacred, consecrated; but on the other hand it means
> uncanny, dangerous, forbidden, and unclean.
> Sigmund Freud, *Totem and Taboo*

During the time of the ancestors of our ancestors, one of the stories people told was about Abchan. Although it hasn't been preserved in any of the great writings, I would still like to tell it to you. As is often the case with stories that have not been written down in an unchangeable form, the story of Abchan has been changed and expanded many times. I myself know two different versions of it, and a certain trustworthy old man told me he had heard a third one. But over the course of his long life, his now elderly mind had been overfilled with wisdom, and consequently he could no longer remember the third story of Abchan. One of the versions of Abchan's story must be true. Perhaps it's the one I'm about to tell you.

Abchan lived at the beginning of the end of the Great Age. It was during that short period of time when the Almighty had stopped speaking to all the people, but sometimes still spoke to the chosen ones. One of the chosen who could hear the Almighty's voice was Abchan. The Almighty visited him in his dreams and guided his steps.

First, the Almighty led Abchan to the sandy Degha Valley and showed him where to dig a well that would have plenty of water even in times of great drought. Then he sent him to the seaside town of Katru, where a beautiful young woman named Taila lived in a fisherman's family; she was to become Abchan's wife.

Abchan always listened to the will of the Almighty, and he always thanked him, because it was good and right. The news of Abchan's devotion and faith had spread even among the people of faraway lands. They spoke of him with admiration in the Thas river delta as well as on the high plateau, all the way to the town of Dursmet.

Abchan frequently went to the temple and made sacrifices. He thought and acted with ease, because he knew that he was living in accordance with the will of the Almighty.

'Do you hear me, Abchan?' the Almighty's voice sounded once more in Abchan's dream. As always, the sleeping man was terror-struck. In his dream he threw himself on to his knees and hid his face in the dust.

'I command you thus,' the voice went on, 'tomorrow you will leave your home in Degha Valley, you will take your wife, your livestock, and all your possessions which can fit on to a two-wheeled cart. You will move to the town of Om-Eri. There you will meet a person named Nasan. If you serve this person with patience and loyalty, salvation awaits you.'

Abchan awoke pale with fear and sweaty from the effort. He shook his sleeping wife by the arm and told her what he had dreamed. At that time, Taila was with child. The baby she was carrying below her heart was supposed to be born soon. But she got up without grumbling and started to pack their belongings for the journey. Abchan rested in bed a little longer, but then he got up and took care of what needed to be done. It never crossed Abchan's or Taila's mind to go against the Almighty's will. They always obeyed, because it was good and right.

The journey to the town of Om-Eri was difficult, and they made slow headway. Despite the fact that Taila was riding on a donkey, they had to make frequent stops, because the child in her womb was restless, and she was worried she would give birth in the middle of the desert. It took them three days to reach Om-Eri. There were many vacant houses in the town, because their owners had recently been killed by the white plague. Abchan sought out the town council elder, who showed him where they could settle down.

That same night came time for Taila to have her child. Abchan ran back to the elder, who showed him where to find a midwife who assisted women in labour. She lived outside the town walls, by the north gate. When Abchan arrived, at first she didn't even want to open the door for him.

'I've never heard of an Abchan, and I don't know your wife either,' she grumbled from behind the closed door.

But Abchan screamed and wailed so loudly that she finally opened the door. Abchan thought he saw a man's silhouette behind her in the hut. He pressed a gold coin into the woman's hand and pushed her in front of him through the dark streets.

As they approached the house, they could hear Taila's cries from afar.

'It's not her first birth, is it?' the midwife asked.

'It is,' Abchan said.

'Why didn't you say so, you dolt?' she yelled, and ran towards the door.

Taila was lying on the floor in a puddle of amniotic fluid. The midwife clasped her hands in a short prayer. Then she asked Abchan for a clean cloth, and sent him to the well for fresh water.

By the time Abchan returned with a full water bag, the midwife was already wrapping a crying child in the cloth. She said:

'You have a son. He's not very strong, but he's not weak either. Your wife is damaged inside. She has to stay in bed for five days. Don't let her get up. Give her goat's milk to drink, so that her body is able to feed the child. And don't even think about going near her as a husband—it would kill her. Now give me another gold coin. I'll come back tomorrow, but you won't have to pay again.'

The next day Abchan took his son to the temple. He brought sacrificial gifts and named his son Nasan. It would always remind him of why the Almighty had sent him to Om-Eri.

The child grew, and Taila recovered. She was even more beautiful than before. But Abchan wasn't happy. When he had been walking through the desert from Degha Valley, he had envisioned a wise, noble old man named Nasan living in this town. Abchan had assumed that his task was to record the old man's wise words on parchment, and to take care of him in his old age up to a dignified death. He was going to serve him with patience and loyalty, as the voice of the Almighty had commanded in his dream. But soon Abchan figured out that no one named Nasan lived in Om-Eri.

During the spring and autumn pilgrimages, many people came to the famous temple in Om-Eri. They wanted to spend the holidays of pasel or riak-dhol in this sacred place. Abchan believed that Nasan was going to be among the pilgrims.

Abchan sowed, took care of livestock, and repaired the house, but all the while he kept counting the days until the holidays and meeting Nasan. The only time he forgot about the duty arising from his dream was when he held his son in his arms. But as soon as he spoke his son's name, he would immediately remember that he had yet to find the real Nasan, and his brow furrowed again. Until that point, he had always felt confident, because he was following the Almighty's commands. But now everything was upside down. There was a command, but he didn't know how to fulfil it. He waited impatiently for the pilgrims to arrive for riak-dhol.

There were also moments when he allowed himself to admit the blasphemous thought that he was afraid of meeting Nasan. Abchan held his son in his arms, and thought about the fact that soon he would have to follow Nasan in order to serve him with loyalty and patience. But what would happen to his wife and son? Taila had always been devoted to him, but she didn't have the strength for a long trip yet, so she couldn't go with him. And what if Nasan ordered Abchan to leave without his family? He'd have to leave his beloved son, his little pink cheeks that had a happy smile whenever he looked at his father; he'd have to leave behind his curious black eyes and unusually blond hair, as fine as wheat flour.

Finally the time of riak-dhol came. Abchan arrived at the temple gate before the guard opened it, and he stayed on the steps until the last pilgrim left that night. He didn't even attend the services so as not to miss Nasan.

'Is there a man named Nasan in your group?' he asked another group of pilgrims for what seemed like the thousandth time.

'My parents named my younger brother Nasan,' an old, white-haired man said.

'Where is he?' Abchan asked with trepidation.

'He died when he was a small child. I'm sure that by now he's looking at the Almighty's face.'

Another time when Abchan asked about Nasan, a young man stood in his way and challenged him.

'My wife's Nasama. What do you want from her?'

On the last day, people from Degha Valley came to the temple. They remembered Abchan, and told him about what had happened since he left. The news was not good. Large packs of famished black wolves had stormed in from the desert. They were attacking livestock as well as people. Not far from Abchan's former home, they had ripped apart Taila's best friend and her child. The pilgrims were trying to decide whether to return to their homes.

The holidays ended, and Nasan still had not come. Abchan asked the priests for advice. He had already spoken to all of them at the temple, but not one of them was able to help him. He noticed that some of them even looked at him as if he were lying or insane. They didn't believe his stories about the Almighty who kept appearing in his dreams. They doubted that the Almighty first led Abchan to the sandy Degha Valley and showed him where to dig a well that would have plenty of water, then sent him to the seaside town of Katru to ask a fisherman for his beautiful daughter Taila's hand in marriage, and finally commanded Abchan to look for someone named Nasan in Om-Eri.

The priests only answered him by repeating traditional wisdom and religious doctrine. The Almighty does not err. If he said that Abchan would meet Nasan in Om-Eri, then that is what would happen. Abchan had free will and could choose how to fulfil the Almighty's command. And finally, all time spent in the temple is good and opens a path to salvation.

Sometimes pilgrims came to the famous temple in Om-Eri even outside the holidays. Although Abchan had made the priests and temple guards promise they'd ask for the name of every stranger that showed up at the temple, he was still anxious. He knew that the guards by the gate were often asleep, and the priests were fully absorbed in the services, so it was possible that Nasan would come and go from the temple and Abchan would never find out about it. The truth of the matter was that the Almighty had tasked him with finding Nasan, not the priests or the guards. It was his job to spend as much time as possible at the temple.

Right before the pasel holidays, Abchan's son Nasan fell ill. He ran a high fever and his tongue had a white coating, like the tongue of someone who had been bitten by a venomous spider. The boy was short of breath and he wheezed like a weak old man. The herbalist said that the only thing which would keep him alive was the red flower of the desert. The child should drink its tea three times a day.

'This sickness often lasts for many years, but if the boy survives to become a man, it will disappear. Until then he has to drink the tea regularly,' the herbalist added, and left them some dried red petals which Taila steeped in boiling water.

Abchan spent the whole day in the desert and found several plants. But then came the holidays, and he had to keep waiting for Nasan at the temple.

On the last day of pasel, Taila tied the child to her hip and went into the desert, because the herbs Abchan had found were gone. She didn't have as much luck as her husband and wasn't able to find the red flower of the desert.

It got dark. She had to spend the night outside with little Nasan. In the middle of the night, the boy broke into a cold sweat, and Taila began to say prayers for the dying child. As the next day was dawning, she saw a cluster of red flowers of the desert nearby. She quickly tore off a flower and let her son suck on it. His condition improved immediately.

When she came back to town, she went to the temple to tell her husband about it. Abchan listened to her absentmindedly. Although pasel had ended, he was still on the lookout for a man named Nasan to walk into the temple. The only thing that stuck in his mind from his wife's tale was the thought of a dead child. Although he couldn't imagine losing his beloved son, he also realised how different things would be if that were to happen. He'd have nothing tying him to everyday life any more, and he could spend his days waiting for Nasan at the temple, morning till night.

Although Abchan's son Nasan was alive, his father had to let him die in his mind. He cut the tie that was binding him to his son and wife, in order to be able to spend day after day, morning till night, in prayer, waiting at the temple gate for his Nasan. Abchan had no doubt that sooner or later that day would come. The voice of the Almighty had told him so.

Loyal Taila occasionally brought her husband a little bit of food or some clean clothes, but her life was very hard. She had to sow, take care of the livestock, and repair the house, but most importantly, she had to keep going out to the desert to get her son the red flowers.

Taila was beautiful. Men always like to help a woman like that. One man brought her some fish, another gave her a ride to the desert on a donkey. Taila was beautiful. Other women always say bad things about a woman like that. One woman complained that she was seducing her husband, another added that strangers were spending the night at her house.

When Abchan left, Taila worked as hard as she could. One after another she sold all the things she and her son didn't need. With the money she earned she bought wheat, milk, or a basket of dates. But one day the money ran out, and there were only a few of the life-giving red petals left in the bag. Taila's lips whispered a prayer. She asked the Almighty for Abchan finally to find Nasan, and for him to be a wealthy man who'd send them a purse of gold coins and the best healer from his retinue to heal her son. There was a banging on her door.

The man who had come was definitely not a messenger of the Almighty. He was a wealthy merchant, a profligate and a debaucher, who was passing through Om-Eri with his caravan. He was looking to have fun with a prostitute, and someone's poisonous tongue had told him he would find one in this house. When he saw the beautiful Taila at the door, passion gleamed in his eyes.

'I'll give you ten gold coins,' he whispered.

'What's your name?' Taila asked, full of hope, still thinking of the name the Almighty had spoken to her husband.

'Call me Batsali,' the man said.

'I want twenty gold coins, Batsali,' Taila said with a disappointed sigh.

From then on Taila had a lot of money and a lot of enemies. She was able to pay a poor widow to go into the desert to pick red flowers, and an orphaned girl to clean her house. One woman's beauty provided sustenance for four hungry mouths.

When Abchan found out that Taila had become a prostitute, it calmed his confused mind. Before, he had often thought about his wife and son, he missed them, and an inexplicable force kept pulling him to leave the temple and live with his family. Now it was no longer possible. He could cast Taila aside without any scruples. Though when the council members reminded him that as the husband he could decide whether Taila should be banished from the town, he told them to let her stay in Om-Eri. Then they asked him whether he wanted them to take away her son. Abchan's heart ached. He said he was giving up little Nasan too, and letting him become the impure child of a prostitute.

And so the boy became an impure child of a prostitute. He grew up alone, far from his mother's carousing, because he quickly came to despise Taila. He only went home for the servant to give him food or his medicinal tea. The only time he spent longer at the house was when his health deteriorated. Otherwise he wandered the town or the desert. He didn't have any friends, because no parents would allow their children to play with the son of a prostitute.

Little Nasan was growing up to be a scoundrel who committed evil deeds for his own entertainment. He stole hens from people's yards in order to burn them alive and laugh at their desperate clucking. If a stray dog crossed his path, he hung it by its legs and stoned it. But more than anything, Nasan hated people. He indulged in the fantasy that when he grew up, he'd barge into Om-Eri at the head of a large army, and personally stab every citizen of the town.

Time passed. Taila's beauty blew away with the desert wind and burned up in the hot sun. Instead of twenty gold coins, she had to settle for two, and sometimes she had to be happy with a piece of cloth or a basket of dried fish. She had no one to give the gold to anyway. And she no longer needed the red flowers of the desert. Her son had survived to become a man, and the sickness vanished. Soon after that, the boy vanished too. Taila was used to the boy wandering off, so it took her a few days to realise that he was gone for good.

Abchan was still waiting for a man named Nasan, whom he could serve with patience and loyalty, and thus open a path to his own salvation. Judging by his age, Abchan wasn't an old man yet, but the long years of standing at the temple gate in the heat of the sun and in sandstorms, together with the nights spent on the cold temple floor, had turned him into a poor wretch with a hunched back, shaky hands, and unruly bowels. What kind of service could he offer Nasan if he were to show up?

One day, news spread across Om-Eri that there were outlaws coming from the west. It was an army of tattered criminals who showed no mercy, which had been making its way from town to town since winter, spreading pain and death. Three times a royal expedition tried to stop them, and three times the scoundrels defeated it. Now they were standing at the gates of Om-Eri, and the council had to decide what to do. The elders knew that there weren't enough battle-trained men in town, and time had ravaged the town walls in many places. That's how it always goes when a period of peace lasts too long.

The council decided that the town would not try to defend itself. The elders were hoping that if the outlaws found the town empty, they'd leave. The citizens were free to decide for themselves. Everyone chose escape. People took their most valuable possessions and ran. In the chaos, husbands were forgetting their wives. Fathers were abandoning their children, and daughters were abandoning their elders. Friends didn't lend each other a helping hand. The people of Om-Eri were on the run. Some were planning to stay with relatives in other lands, others wanted to wait in the desert until the danger had passed. But most of them didn't have a destination. Escape was their destination.

Fear of the outlaws was enormous. All the townspeople had gathered by the eastern gate. There were children, old people, men and women with camels, horses, donkeys, and carts. There was moaning and wailing, there were tears as well as blood; people sustained many injuries, as if the outlaw army had already arrived in town.

Taila did not leave. She didn't hear about the threat to the town. No law-abiding citizen would enter the house of a prostitute, and the ones who used to frequent her house had other things to worry about. Taila heard noise from the street, and she opened her shutters a bit, concerned that a group of angry wives might be coming to her home, as had happened a few times in the past. But she saw that no one was threatening her house.

She became more concerned when the whole town grew quiet all of a sudden. There were none of the sounds the human ear is accustomed to. No talking, laughter, quarrels, or crying. Worried, Taila walked out on to the empty street. She peeked through windows and called into yards. But she found no one. Like anyone who wanders around aimlessly, she ended up in the town square. She saw that the large temple gate, which remained open even on fast days, was closed. And then she heard a ruckus coming from the western gate. It was the shouting of men mixed with the sound of horses' hooves. Taila looked in that direction. A cloud of swirling dust appeared over the rooftops.

The front line of the outlaw army galloped into the square, shouting. The men halted their horses and looked around nervously, waiting to see from which side the defenders' arrows would start falling on them. When they realised that the town wasn't mounting a defence, they sheathed their swords and daggers and laughed diabolically. Then a woman by the temple gate caught their eye.

Their eyes, which hadn't seen a woman's body for a long time, glistened with animal lust.

'Leave her for the chief,' one of the commanders shouted, but his voice was drowned out by the men's lustful panting and whooping. Those who had been relegated to satisfying their urges on mares for a long time could now get hold of a woman. A woman who was still alive.

By the time the main unit of the outlaw army led by the chief made it to Om-Eri, some of the houses were already in flames. The chief headed straight for the square. He had often heard that there was a lot of gold at the temple, and now the whole fortune was within his reach. He himself did not desire gold or precious stones, but he had a plan to divide it up in a manner that would bind some of his commanders to him even more strongly, and make the others want to serve him all the more loyally. The strength of his army was built on competition, jealousy, and hate.

'Break down the gate,' the chief ordered as he stepped over a man who was satisfying himself on a limp woman's body on the steps.

The bandits' axes started to chop into the old cedar wood. It was hard work. The exalted work of art made by the ancient temple builders resisted the unclean hands of the criminals for a long time. Teams attempting to take down the temple gate had to swap out a dozen times. The impatient chief propelled the tired warriors with a whip. Finally the gate came crashing down. The men ran inside.

'Stop,' the chief of the outlaws yelled. He wanted to enter the temple alone so that he could examine the treasure that was hidden inside.

'Are you Nasan?' a hunched old man asked the chief and stood in his way.

'Yes, I'm Nasan, who was cast aside by his own father, Abchan, even though he was supposed to serve him with patience and loyalty,' the chief said, and he lopped off the old man's head.

This, then, was one of the versions of the story of Abchan, whom the voice of the Almighty had commanded to serve a man named Nasan with patience and loyalty. Perhaps this version is the most widespread among the people because it features things that many people are secretly drawn to: prostitutes, undefeatable criminals, and eccentrics who abandon their families.

But there is another way to tell the story. The introduction stays the same as in the first version. Abchan lived at the beginning of the end of the Great Age. It was during that short period of time when the Almighty had stopped speaking to all the people, but sometimes still spoke to the chosen ones. One of the chosen who could hear the Almighty's voice was Abchan. The Almighty visited him in his dreams and guided his steps.

First, the Almighty led Abchan to the sandy Degha Valley and showed him where to dig a well that would have plenty of water even in times of great drought. Then he sent him to the seaside town of Katru, where a beautiful young woman named Taila lived in a fisherman's family; she was to become Abchan's wife.

Abchan always listened to the will of the Almighty, and he always thanked him, because it was good and right. He frequently went to the temple and made sacrifices. He thought and acted with ease, because he knew that he was living in accordance with the will of the Almighty.

Then, just like in the first version of the story, the Almighty commanded Abchan:

'Tomorrow you will leave your home in Degha Valley, you will take your wife, your livestock, and all your possessions which can fit on to a two-wheeled cart. You will move to the town of Om-Eri. There you will meet a person named Nasan. If you serve this person with patience and loyalty, salvation awaits you.'

The journey to the town of Om-Eri was difficult, and they made slow headway. At that time, Taila was with child, just like in the first version of the story. Despite the fact that Taila was riding on a donkey, they had to make frequent stops, because the child in her womb was restless, and she was worried she would give birth in the middle of the desert. It took them three days to reach Om-Eri. There were many vacant houses in the town, because their owners had recently been killed by the white plague. Abchan sought out the town council elder, who showed him where they could settle down. That same night came time for Taila to have her child. The next day Abchan took his son to the temple. He brought sacrificial gifts and named his son Nasan. It would always remind him of why the Almighty had sent him to Om-Eri.

The child grew, and Taila recovered. But Abchan wasn't happy. When he had been walking through the desert from Degha Valley, he had envisioned a wise, noble old man named Nasan living in this town. But soon he figured out that no one named Nasan lived in Om-Eri.

During the spring and autumn pilgrimages, many people came to the famous temple in Om-Eri. Abchan believed that Nasan was going to be among the pilgrims. First came the pasel holidays, followed by riak-dhol. Abchan spoke to the pilgrims, but none of them was called Nasan.

Until that point, he had always felt confident, because he was following the Almighty's commands. But now everything was upside down. There was a command, but he didn't know how to fulfil it. Since pilgrims came to the famous temple in Om-Eri even outside the holidays, Abchan wanted to spend as much time as possible there.

Then Abchan's son Nasan fell ill. Although the symptoms of the ailment were the same as in the first version of the story—that is, high fever, a white coating on his tongue, and wheezing—this is where the stories diverge. When the herbalist said that the only thing which would keep the child alive was the tea made from the red flower of the desert, Abchan spent several days praying, soul-searching, and fasting, and he decided to fight for his child's life. Although he couldn't imagine losing his beloved son, he also realised how different things would be if that were to happen. If his son Nasan did not survive, it would be a sign from the Almighty that he should go to the temple for good and search for the real Nasan. But while his son was alive, Abchan was going to stay with him.

Abchan sowed, took care of the livestock, repaired the house, and went into the desert to pick the red flower. At the same time he was racked with guilt, because at any moment Nasan could have come into the temple, prayed, and then left for ever.

Desperate, Abchan prayed that the Almighty would guide him to meet Nasan, or that he would speak to him again in a dream and tell him clearly what to do. But in his mind Abchan knew that the Almighty would not be coming back to explain the meaning of his earlier words.

Whenever his son's condition deteriorated, Abchan stopped praying to meet Nasan and begged the Almighty for his child's life.

Time passed. Taila's beauty blew away with the desert wind and burned up in the hot sun. The long years of searching for the red flower of the desert in the heat of the sun and in sandstorms had turned Abchan into a poor wretch with a hunched back, shaky hands, and unruly bowels. Their son Nasan survived and reached the first signs of adulthood. But instead of the relief that the herbalist had predicted years earlier, his health suddenly deteriorated. In order to be able to breathe, he had to drink a lot more of the medicinal tea than ever before.

Abchan had to search the desert every day from morning till night. He only came home when he had enough red flowers in his backpack. His heart commanded him to fight for his son's health, and even the news that a group of outlaws was wandering near Om-Eri did not deter him.

He didn't think about the outlaws, and when they surrounded him in a dark gorge, he realised how long it had been since he had thought about Nasan, the man the Almighty's voice had told him about so long ago, and whom he was supposed to serve with patience and loyalty. The criminals who captured Abchan committed evil deeds for their own entertainment. When they saw that Abchan was a poor man who had nothing they could take, it made them all the more cruel. They beat him, cut him, and hacked at him until they got tired.

But Abchan didn't die right away. His eyes opened for a moment. He got a glimpse of the face of his beloved son, who was bending over him and washing his wounds. When his son saw that Abchan had come to, he whispered:

'Father, can you hear me? It's me, your son, Nasan. I am healed. You'll never have to go back to the desert for the red flowers.'

Abchan exhaled for the last time. He didn't hear the rest of his son's words, which went like this:

'Father, accept this thanks from your son, Nasan, whom you have served for many years with patience and loyalty.'

These are the two versions of the story of Abchan and Nasan. In one, Abchan abandons his family and lives his entire life confident that he's fulfilling the will of the Almighty, but right before his death he realises that he had been mistaken. In the other, he doesn't fulfil the will of the Almighty, but prioritises his love for his family, and he dies knowing that he had done the right thing.

'What matters more, good intentions or good deeds? In the end, which of these two Abchans was saved?' you might ask.

I too was troubled by such questions when I was young. Priests answered me by repeating traditional wisdom and religious doctrine. The Almighty does not err. If he said that Abchan would meet Nasan in Om-Eri, then that is what must have happened. Abchan had free will and could choose how to fulfil the Almighty's command. Time spent in the temple and love for your fellow man are good. And, one very old interpreter of the writings added, the Almighty is infinitely compassionate and opens a path to salvation for everyone.

On the Other Side of the Mountain Range,
on the Opposite Bank of the River

> For you the days are a succession of sounds, some distinct,
> some almost imperceptible; you have learned to distinguish
> them, to evaluate their provenance and their distance…
> Italo Calvino, 'A King Listens'

Your Most Exalted Majesty, Emperor of the Land and King of Its People, this letter is from Umbras, the son of his father Uraten and his mother Distrimoda, your faithful servant and admirer, who stands today with one foot over the grave and the other already in it, constantly asking the Almighty Creator and Fair Judge for blessings for you and your empire. Your servant Umbras dares to write you this letter, because he wants it to celebrate the infinite wisdom and boundless goodness of your reign for future generations.

Your Most Exalted Majesty, while writing this letter Umbras is aware that his words will not reach you, because he is familiar with the order of life in the palace, where, via readers, his words will first reach the ears of the third-level advisers, who may select it for readers of the second-level advisers, but those will certainly not recommend Umbras's words to the first-level advisers, sending them instead to be preserved in the archives. With his head bowed, your loyal servant Umbras admits that this is his goal, because he knows that according to one of your astute royal decrees, every letter addressed directly to you, like the one Umbras is now writing with greatest humility, must be preserved in the archives, in a dry and mild breeze, somewhere beneath the cellars and crypts. Thanks to this enlightened decree, the words in my letter will be accessible in one year just as they will be in a thousand. It is for the listeners of the reader who will pick up this letter in a thousand years that Umbras is giving his testimony, in which he describes the endless wisdom and the boundless kindness of Your Most Exalted Majesty, Emperor of the Land and King of Its People.

Many years of life have gnarled Umbras's fingers, but he is using them to pick up a quill in order to describe the strange events of his life. Umbras apologises profusely for his nigh-on unreadable handwriting, shaky from all the things that advanced age brings. Cramps twist Umbras's words, coughing fits make his lines skip around, and chills make them shiver. Death is stretching its powerful claws towards Umbras, and he must fear the anger of the Fair Judge, towards whom he is getting unmistakably closer every day. Other men of Umbras's age have a scribe summoned to dictate their last will to him in accordance with wise imperial decrees about property, dividing up their livestock, fields, or houses in the fairest manner, or deciding the fate of their unmarried sons and daughters. At least in this matter Umbras can be at peace, for he has no livestock, fields, houses, sons, or daughters, so he has no way to cause injustice. For that, Umbras is grateful to the Almighty Creator and Fair Judge.

Your Most Exalted Majesty, forgive Umbras the unsightly slant of his letters, for he has not written anything for a very long time. Even now, after his urgent pleas have grown into insistent wailing, he has only been handed a small papyrus scroll and an oft-used quill. Umbras is well able to judge the jaggedness of his lines, and he is ashamed of it, for he too used to be a scribe. He used to say that if a person is not able to write, there is no shame in it, because he could still learn to do so, but if a person has unsightly handwriting he is insulting his readers and teachers, and most importantly, he is sinning against the Almighty Creator and Fair Judge, who has endowed him with the gift of writing.

Your Most Exalted Majesty, Emperor of the Land and King of Its People, your loyal servant Umbras is aware that he is offending you by writing so much about himself. He begs you on his knees to forgive him. Never before has there been a direct connection between Umbras's writing hand and his heart or mind, he has never written about himself, he swears to you that he has never devoted a single line to himself or his deeds, and that is the reason he is so confused now. He finds himself in an endless loop, worrying about the clarity of his words, but his worry further diminishes their clarity.

Umbras knows how to write because his kind parents, Uraten and Distrimoda, afforded him an education; they did not hesitate to spend their last zekham on teachers. Umbras repaid his parents and teachers by being a patient and humble student, eagerly mastering the art of the embellished style of lovers, the humble tone of entreaties, as well as the terse exactitude of business correspondence and contracts. Before reaching the age of seventeen, he had a scribe's stand at the market in the lower town, and silver zekhams accumulated in the purse on his belt, because people came to see him when they needed to send an entreaty to a tax collector or an urgent message to a husband on a distant business trip. It was a rare occurrence for Umbras to sit in his stand without work, but whenever it happened, he was able to make use of the time to observe and listen to the market women around him. They were women from the hot South, simple and pure of heart like children, who spoke Pte among themselves. People are convinced that it is a difficult language for us, almost impossible, but that is not true. We have many words in common, undoubtedly, our languages separated in the fog of the distant past like branches growing from the same tree; therefore, if a person of our land sets aside his prejudice and pays close attention to the people from the South, watching their slow but meticulous movements, reading the corners of their always smiling mouths and the glint of their curious eyes, if he puts himself in the minds of the people from the South, searching for the reasons for the wrinkles on their foreheads or their hand gestures the way Umbras has done, he will learn Pte relatively quickly. Umbras himself is proof of it, because after only one year he was able to write letters and contracts in Pte. From that point on, he became an almost wealthy man, because commerce between people from our lowlands and the provinces in the South was blossoming during Umbras's youth.

With the awe due the Almighty Creator and Fair Judge, as well as with all due respect to you, Your Most Exalted Majesty, Emperor of the Land and King of Its People, with his head bowed Umbras must admit that he was a good scribe; after all, the word of his craft had slipped all the way under the gates of the imperial palace. After a few years, though not too many, because Umbras was still a young man who was starting to think about his future and not just dream about it, he was summoned to the imperial palace. It happened in the two-hundred-and-seventh year after the destructive flood, during the time of the first harvest of rice and legumes. Besides enormous respect for the Emperor of the Land and King of Its People, Umbras also felt a mustard seed's worth of satisfaction, because his craft was being recognised. Umbras showed the summons with the ruler's seal to the guard at the gate with a light blush on his face and without the slightest worry, because back then rumours had not yet started to spread about people disappearing after being taken away by the trusted Imperial Guard, never to be seen again. Umbras would not have believed such rumours anyway, nor would he have listened to them; he would have yelled at the gossiper and got away from him. Every day Umbras woke up and fell asleep with a sense of peace and security known only to those who have nothing to fear, because they do not know what it feels like to violate age-old rules of public and private morals or go against imperial decrees, they have never criticised or ridiculed royal decisions, nor have they spread other gossip or writing unfriendly towards the ruler or the land. Even when, in the hot afternoon sun, men intoxicated by young wine dictated letters whose words could have concealed sedition or objections to the established order, he knew how to temper those words, to dull a potential thorn, to organise them into sentences in such a manner that neither the sender nor the recipient of the letter written in Umbras's hand would ever face any investigation or punishment. He subordinated his craft to this honourable goal, first and foremost out of respect and love for the Emperor of the Land and King of Its People—that was the real reason he would never write down anything which would so much as hint at betrayal of you, Your Most Exalted Majesty.

In the palace, Umbras was taken to the first of the emperor's secretaries. That educated and experienced man tested him on the main arts of the scribe—speed of writing words with closed eyes, speed of taking dictation blindfolded, fluency of recitation, and accuracy of mathematical calculations. That same afternoon, Umbras learned from the mouth of the first imperial secretary that he was to become a third-level court scribe. What honour and glory for a young man, whose kind parents, Uraten and Distrimoda, were just ordinary poor people living off the work of their hands. Aware of his responsibility to the Emperor of the Land and King of Its People, Umbras fulfilled his duties with zeal and exactitude, so that a year later he became a second-level court scribe. In the green offices on the third floor of the lower palace, where the second-level court scribes sit behind their small desks, Umbras was again able to fulfil all the tasks his superiors assigned to him without mistakes or delays. In the two-hundred-and-twelfth year after the destructive flood, during the time of the harvest of grapes and late dates, those prudent men decided that Umbras was to become a scribe and reader to the Emperor of the Land and King of Its People. To this day Umbras does not know how he became deserving of this honour, since in the ranks of the second-level court scribes there were several who were famous for their speed and accuracy. If Umbras, now an old man with one eye looking into a dug grave and the other looking up from the depths of said grave, dared judge this decision, he would surmise that what had weighed in his favour was what has long been referred to as the leopard harmony of the scribe's art—that is, the combination of speed and accuracy in writing.

Yes, Your Most Exalted Majesty, Emperor of the Land and King of Its People, this letter is from your faithful servant Umbras, the young scribe, who when he was first introduced to you a long time ago, tripped over the threshold of the day chamber, and instead of kneeling, he sprawled out in front of Your Most Exalted Majesty. He can still remember your heartfelt, resounding laughter. The guards immediately wanted to take Umbras away and punish him, the commander of the Iron Shield had already given the order with his right hand, but Your Most Exalted Majesty's extended left arm stopped them. The new scribe may have been saved by your youth, which even in the case of the highest rulers and dignitaries is still inclined towards gaiety and spontaneity, that later give way to prudence and re-strained determination. At least that is what the wise scrolls say about the expected development of the surge of human emotions and minds. As Umbras is arranging these words into lines, he realises that he is relying on generalisations, which authors rightfully make in their scrolls, instead of on the uniqueness that already distinguished the spirit of Your Most Exalted Majesty back then, even though in physical age and length of reign you were a young Emperor of the Land and King of Its People. Since the time of the destructive flood, our land has never had such a young ruler, and it is possible that even long before that horrible event no one physically younger than Your Most Exalted Majesty had sat on the throne, since our knowledge of times past is not rooted in the memory of scrolls, but only in the untrustworthy repetition of that which has been transmitted from lips to ears, which often results in fairy-tale-like stories rather than family trees and didactical tales. Judge for yourself, Your Most Exalted Majesty, how much one can believe the story of the Silver Child, whom a giant sea eagle let down from its talons on to the throne, or the story of the Rainbow Child, who was born on the throne from the sun's rays after the end of the Age of Rain. These stories are very popular among our people, storytellers at market-places tell them to the young and old for a fee, and mothers tell them to their children before they fall asleep, but what is troublesome about them is that even though they contradict our religion, being mutually exclusive with the faith in the uniqueness of the Almighty Creator and Fair Judge, our priests and wise men in the temples do not discredit these fairy tales; in fact, Umbras can remember several occasions on which some principle of faith, morals, or existence was being explained at the temple on the basis of such stories.

Your Most Exalted Majesty, even though in physical age and length of rule you were a very young Emperor of the Land and King of Its People, you had none of the qualities that the scrolls consider widespread among young rulers. You were never frivolous or rash, nor moody or flighty. You never had the fomented blood of youth, which desires glory and victories, or worse yet, blood and the wailing of the vanquished. Under your sceptre, our land enjoyed a calm and balanced life, like the flow of the mighty river Medalamur in the western lowlands. But you, Your Most Exalted Majesty, were neither calm nor content. You dictated many decrees for officials, administrators, and commanders, in which you asked them to fight more effectively against all expressions of injustice and evil in our land. When your humble servant Umbras read Your Most Exalted Majesty their obliging, though confused answers, your sighs and occasional exclamations of disagreement made it clear that you were not happy with your empire. You wanted to eliminate not only murder, robbery, and theft, classified as crimes of raging malice, but also speculation, property fraud, and physical or emotional infidelity, which are the most common crimes of smouldering malice, and furthermore, you also intended to root out disrespect for old age and inadequate maternal or paternal care, which are sins in the eyes of the Almighty Creator and Fair Judge, but do not have a separate label in the scrolls of the Law of Princess Hordona, which has been governing our empire for over a century. You were young of body, but you wanted to rule a caring empire enlightened by good. Unfortunately, day after day you encountered resistance from the dignitaries who, while serving you and the law, were trying to understand the scrolls bearing your orders and decrees only with their minds, even though they should have relied more on their hearts. In one short scroll you asked them what the purpose of the trusted Imperial Guard was and whether they could imagine running their province or district without it, but the confused replies that came back from those diligent men made Your Most Exalted Majesty all the more frustrated.

Umbras must admit that he does not know whether it is still the case today, Your Most Exalted Majesty, Emperor of the Land and King of Its People, but he can clearly remember that in your youth you were an avid hunter. While in the corridors of the royal palace one could occasionally hear the echoes of malicious whispers that the Emperor and King was cooling his boiling young blood on dangerous hunts, one—perhaps the only one—of your humble servants suspected that there could be a different explanation. That servant was Umbras, who is now asking you, Your Most Exalted Majesty, to show mercy, and to allow him to hint at his past conjectures. He will not succeed in expressing them exactly, because he is but an old man, with one ear listening to funeral dirges, and the other having already heard the last of them, attempting to unravel the threads of his memory for the last time, in order to uncover what he thought many years ago, but never confided to a soul back then or since. Thoughts are like that; if they remain unsaid, they remain unclear, because if a thought does not make it into words, it has no means of achieving exactness and purity; a thought hidden in one's head is wrapped in noise, through which even the ears growing out of the same head cannot make anything out.

Umbras, aware of his mistakes and imperfect judgement, thinks that in times past Your Most Exalted Majesty was seeking out the thrill and pleasure of the hunt not to show off his equestrian skill while chasing a deer, or the accuracy of his shooting at a target the size of a swallow, but to escape from his office for a few moments or days, to get a respite from the irreversible fate that had placed him on the throne of the land, which, to the outside observer, was flourishing and enjoyed the respect of its allies as well as its enemies, but in the eyes of its young Emperor of the Land and King of Its People was full of injustice and malice, which even this strong and esteemed ruler was not able to correct. Umbras will never forget a particular moment—it took place after he finished writing a long scroll to the royal administrator of sugar and salt—when Your Most Exalted Majesty asked your humble scribe how it was possible that some people would choose the fate of a petty market thief of their own free will, others could become husbands and fathers of beautiful children and then spend their zekhams on prostitutes, and still others would achieve the office of imperial collector, but besides filling the purse of the land, would also fill their own purse. At that moment Umbras was not blindfolded—the scroll to the royal administrator of sugar and salt was not considered a palace secret. He glanced in the direction of the face of the Emperor of the Land and King of Its People, and before he bowed respectfully, he got a glimpse of the ruler's curious eyes. Even with all due respect for the nobility of Your Most Exalted Majesty, your humble servant and admirer was able to surmise that the Emperor of the Land and King of Its People had a genuine interest in the scribe's thoughts; his father Uraten and mother Distrimoda would never have dared so much as to hope that there would come a moment in the life of their son Umbras when he would be asked to share his opinion with the ruler himself. The humble imperial scribe proved his worth as a humble imperial scribe, confirming he was nothing more, only the intermediary for the thoughts of others; he stammered, whispering that he did not know the answer, he did not know why some people would choose the fate of a petty market thief of their own free will, he did not understand how others could become husbands and fathers of beautiful children and then spend their zekhams on prostitutes, and he did not understand the reason why still others would achieve the office of imperial collector, but besides filling the purse of the land, would also fill their own purse.

Your Most Exalted Majesty often dictated to Umbras orders which charged the palace chamberlain and the commander of the Imperial Guard with preparations for multi-day expeditions into sparsely populated mountains, forests, deserts, or steppes of your far-flung empire. In this manner you got to know your empire, but you were more Emperor of the Land, the stretch of territory, than King of Its People, those sinful souls whose malice and pettiness deserved your contempt, which never came, because Your Most Exalted Majesty thought about lifting the poor souls out of their pettiness and malice rather than about the just punishment they would have deserved. Without the slightest hesitation, Umbras, who has read many lines, can declare that no scroll preserved in the archives describes such a merciful and kind ruler, and therefore, your humble servant and loyal admirer can gladly ask the Almighty Creator and Fair Judge for a blessing for you and your empire.

Your Most Exalted Majesty's favourite places to hunt were in the northern provinces, in the wild and dangerous places bounded by the precipices of the Iklabe mountain range and the wild torrent of the river Plamur. On one memorable day, or to be exact, in one memorable moment, Your Most Exalted Majesty gave the order to drive the horses through the wild torrent of the river Plamur, then to dismount and climb the treacherous rocky walls of the Iklabe mountain range on foot. Umbras can picture the moment: the air was moist and crisp, because the mist rising from the wild river was mixing with the cold gusts of mountain wind, the members of Your Most Exalted Majesty's retinue had their clothes soaked in sweat, the corners of their mouths were drooping from exhaustion, and the dark shadows of fear showed in their eyes; the horses bucked at the sight of the raging current, their animal instinct preventing them from stepping into danger; the prudent commander of the Iron Shield pointed out to your Majesty that on the opposite bank of the river Plamur you would no longer be the Emperor of the Land, but a stranger in completely unexplored territory; he reiterated his objection with greater insistence when you gave the order to climb the peaks of the Iklabe mountain range, on the other side of which could await a dangerous world full of unfamiliar kinds of animals, among which could be giant predators or deadly venomous reptiles or scorpions, not to mention hordes of savages or wolf people, but your Majesty's decision was immutable, as a ruler's decision must always be. Umbras was a scribe and reader to the Emperor of the Land and King of Its People; he had not seen any of the things described in the previous lines with his own eyes, he had never experienced the icy chill of the river Plamur, his hands had not been scraped on the sharp edges of the rocks that covered the Iklabe mountain range. He had not feared for his life, which was a recompense for those whom the soldiers ridiculed as being the rear ends of the land, but at the same time Umbras must add that he did not get to experience the sight of the endless green meadow on the other side. To this day Umbras is sad that he did not get to see the very first flash of excitement on the face of Your Most Exalted Majesty when a heretofore-unknown land opened up before him. The hunt then became an expedition of exploration and travel, which in turn became an expedition of conquest, even though there was no one to conquer, because on the opposite bank of the river Plamur and on the other side of the Iklabe mountain range there were no human habitations; the wealth of that beautiful land was not home to any people or empire, therefore Your Most Exalted Majesty was able to subjugate it without shooting a single arrow.

Umbras was among the first to learn about all this when you came back from the expedition, which, for the listeners of the readers of future generations, is a more apt name for it than a hunt. You had barely put away your bow and quiver with the green imperial arrows, and you refused to take off the tight leather hunting outfit, which showed off every muscle of your body and every taut tendon, because you immediately had to dictate several important letters. Your humble servant Umbras was summoned to write an extremely urgent and top-secret letter to the imperial administrator of fields and supplies. As on other such important occasions, Umbras had to write blindfolded with a silk scarf, so that he could not read what Your Most Exalted Majesty was dictating. But before the imperial servant blindfolded him, Umbras noticed the excitement and bliss in your otherwise calm, though more and more frequently disappointed, face. That day Your Most Exalted Majesty's cheeks burned with passion, your eyes blazed with hope, in the corners of your mouth there was a happy, victorious smile, and your voice exuded enthusiasm and fervent joy. After one is blindfolded, the other senses become keener, especially one's hearing, thus Your Most Exalted Majesty's words were not the only things entering Umbras with your voice, he was also flooded with your joy and enthusiasm. Your scribe understood that this was a unique moment, the first of the defining moments of your reign, when you experienced and immediately comprehended something exceptional; you had been enlightened by an idea. In your letter, you informed the imperial administrator of fields and supplies that on the other side of the river Plamur and the Iklabe mountain range, in the territory that had been unknown and uninhabited because of its inaccessibility, but which was now part of our land because a flag with the symbols of Your Most Exalted Majesty had been planted there, you had discovered a vast lowland overgrown with verdant greenery and beautiful flowers, which indicated that the area was not plagued by burning droughts nor by freezing snowstorms, therefore it was suitable for imminent cultivation. You asked the administrator to begin preparations for burning the sparse local forests and for growing agricultural crops as well as fruit trees, you ordered the tilling of the land as soon as possible, and the planting of wheat, barley, hops, and vegetables. However, Your Most Exalted Majesty wisely left it up to the imperial administrator of fields and supplies to decide the specific types of plants based on the make-up, colour, and texture of the local soil, applying his own knowledge and following the counsel of experts.

Umbras is convinced that during the dictation of this letter, a magnificent, timeless plan was forming in the mind of Your Most Exalted Majesty, a plan which will be for ever inscribed into the history of our land, and into the history of all the people of the world. Although the interpreters of the Holy scrolls, priests, and scholars have always argued about the role of the Almighty Creator in our daily life, the degree to which he intrudes or interferes in it versus just observing and recording our deeds, and how much he listens to our prayers and lets us know the decisions of the Fair Judge even in this life, Umbras—with respect in his heart for Eternity and Divine Providence—is thoroughly convinced that Your Most Exalted Majesty's plan was not only forming with the approval of, but had been directly received from the Almighty Creator, who must have entered the hearing of our young Emperor of the Land and King of Its People somewhere on the opposite bank of the river Plamur and the other side of the Iklabe mountain range.

Right after the letter to the imperial administrator of fields and supplies, you started to dictate a message addressed to the principal royal builder. You requested that a wide and solid bridge be built over the wild river Plamur, so that caravans and cargo wagons with the heaviest of loads could flow across to the other side. Furthermore, you tasked the principal royal builder with sending his foremen under the Iklabe peaks to find places through which a road could be carved to the other side of the mountain range. Finally, you assigned him to draw up plans to build a vast city, combining the most beautiful with the most practical elements of construction. The city was to be surrounded by thick, tall walls which could protect about as many citizens as lived in our capital; consequently, rumours soon started to spread through the land that the Emperor of the Land and King of Its People had decided to move his residence to the newly discovered world. But Your Most Exalted

Majesty's plan was incomparably greater in its scope, larger in its intent, and deeper in its goals. That very first day you named the territory, but the name of the newly annexed province of Plamikia did not boom with the wild torrent of the river Plamur with all its treacherous eddies and water-falls, nor did it howl with the icy gale on the peaks of the Iklabe mountain range; the melody of this word conveyed the rustling of a moist breeze over the yet-to-be-planted vineyards and the echoes of children's feet stomping on the cobblestones of the future city square.

The days and months that followed became a time of exhausting preparations for something monumental. You dictated more letters than ever before to your humble servant Umbras. You sent orders to the royal administrator of craftsmen, the main overseer of mines and springs, the first-level librarian, and to the commanders of military districts and regions. Your humble servant marvelled at what a perfect Emperor of the Land and King of Its People you were, because you knew your land like the palm of your hand, and your orders asked of the dignitaries, builders, workers, craftsmen, miners, farmers, shepherds, and soldiers exactly as much as they knew and were able to deliver at any given moment. The King did not ask his people for the impossible, thus the Emperor got from his land everything that was possible. In some interpretation of the Holy scrolls, this could be considered a miracle, a visible intervention of the Almighty Creator in earthly affairs. With expediency exactly corresponding to the highest production potential of the country, a large city with surrounding farmers' and shepherds' settlements was growing on the opposite bank of the wild torrents of the river Plamur and behind the windswept peaks of the Iklabe mountain range. Your Most Exalted Majesty ordered streets to be built in Plamikia consisting of houses, craftsmen's workshops, barracks, palaces, squares with buildings for imperial administration, archives, schools, and temples. Then you ordered to have these buildings outfitted with furniture and tools according to their purpose. Along the newly built road, which led from our capital, straight as a draughtsman's ruler, to the newly built bridge across the river Plamur, to then slowly wind its way up the mountain passes of the Iklabe mountain range, flowed endless caravans of elephants, camels, and horse-drawn wagons laden with all manner of things: couches, chests of drawers, chairs, armchairs, carpets, curtains, tubs, pots, pitchers, pans, and strainers. Our country lived as if in a fever; it was bewildered, as if Your Most Exalted Majesty's enthusiasm had turned into a contagion, which quickly spread among all strata of the population, among the children and the elderly, officials, builders, craftsmen, and people working the land. Every citizen worked with the utmost dedication; the word Plamikia became akin to an incantation of one of the old religions, it gave strength to people as well as to pack animals, it swept away disagreements and misunderstandings, overcame the adversity of the forces of nature, it removed all obstacles. Though at this point Umbras must mention that many of those who participated in this great endeavour also had a selfish vision of a future life in the newly established province, may the

Fair Judge not hold it against them at their final reckoning, because the temptation was extremely great. Everyone who had the good fortune to have been there described the new city and its surroundings as the heavenly realm descended to earth. Umbras can only rely on the observing eyes and describing lips of others in this matter—that is, on the combination of enthrallment and exaggeration—since he himself has never been to Plamikia, he had never asked for permission to go there, even though he would have likely been granted it, because at that time, Your Most Exalted Majesty bestowed your trust and favour upon him, dictating several of the key orders and decrees to him.

By then, Umbras, a humble servant and admirer of Your Most Exalted Majesty, was already living in the lower palace, where the spacious bedroom of the scribes was located. Unlike most of them, he was able to sleep on a soft bed separated from the rest by a curtain, he had his own wash basin for personal hygiene, which, together with the pay of a dozen zekhams for a day's work, was a great honour bestowed only upon a trio of imperial scribes and readers. Even though Umbras was the youngest of the three, which was the reason he did not get summoned to record the secret meetings of Your Most Exalted Majesty, from the more or less clear hints in the conversations of the other two imperial scribes and readers, who, unfortunately, in that manner often exhibited behaviour unbecoming of the office entrusted to them, Umbras not only found out that such meetings took place, but he gathered that in addition to what was being planned in Plamikia—that is, in addition to the endeavour the entire land and all its people were participating in—there existed at the highest level, between the ruler and his most trusted dignitaries, another, undoubtedly more radical and significant plan. At the secret meetings, to which the aforementioned imperial scribes were always summoned abruptly and unexpectedly, but always in the early morning hours, decisions were made that would define the direction of our empire for the coming years, or even decades. When a soldier of the Iron Shield shook sleeping Umbras's arm one cold morning, your humble servant was overcome by fear, excitement, and curiosity. He silently followed the soldier down the empty corridors of a sleeping palace, with all manner of expectations swarming in his head like bees in a hive. Umbras thought he might have to take another oath of silence and loyalty to the Emperor of the Land and King of Its People before taking the secret notes, but everything was as usual, except for the fact that he was not blindfolded by an imperial servant, who was no doubt still asleep, but by the soldier of the Iron Shield who had brought him there. That morning the Emperor of the Land and King of Its People had summoned an older man whose voice Umbras had never heard before—and now, when the humble imperial servant can smell the soil of a freshly dug grave in one nostril, and his other nostril is already clogged by that soil, one could add that he will never hear that man's voice again. With insistence that was in stark contrast to what would be considered appropriate respect for a ruler, the man suggested, even demanded that construction in Plamikia be slowed down, because the land was exhausted and the people were grumbling, which could threaten or even ruin the whole plan. In spite of this man's inappropriate tone, which warranted immediate and severe punishment, Your Most Exalted Majesty replied with a calm and mild demeanour. You assured the man that the preparations were coming to a close; they would be completed that year, at the latest before the stormy season. But the man had so much sinful courage that he kept raising objections, because he thought the stormy season was too far off. Umbras tried to capture every word of the polemic in the lines of the scroll, because no matter how crazy it may sound, the man was having a polemical discussion with the ruler, which at times turned into—may Umbras be forgiven for using the word—an argument, when the Emperor and the man spoke very fast and interrupted each other's words like thunder interrupts a sleeping man's rest, therefore the quill of the poor imperial scribe was not able to capture all of it, but perhaps his mistake was in trying to capture all of it, every single word, including ones that did not lead to a complete thought, instead of concentrating on the most important content and overall meaning of the conversation. In the scribe's art, most of the time the perfection of the whole ensues from the perfection of the smallest parts, but those were different circumstances, and Umbras did not adapt to them in an appropriate manner, or more accurately, he did not adapt to them at all, which was probably the reason why he was never again summoned to take notes at a secret meeting.

Your Most Exalted Majesty, Emperor of the Land and King of Its People, Umbras is about to describe events, the meaning and scope of which he never quite grasped with his simple mind of a scribe, albeit an imperial scribe; he always had to resort to assumptions which took into account gossip he had overheard as well as other people's conjectures, which is why it is possible that not every line he writes will be a true description of reality, but Umbras, appealing to the ears of the Almighty Creator and Fair Judge, swears that what he writes, in best faith and clearest memory, is consistent with what he thought in those days and what he still thinks now, when he is an old man, who has one arm slipping into his grave clothes, and the other already wrapped in them.

When the new city with its surrounding settlements was nearly built in Plamikia, the fruit trees and the bushes had already been planted, the vegetables had already sprouted from the fertile soil, the storehouses were overflowing, the granaries were full of wheat and rice that had been brought in, and barrels of wine and oils awaited in cellars, a directive of the highest order came from the Emperor of the Land and King of Its People, recalling all the builders, workers, craftsmen, and administrators, that is, everyone who had thus far contributed to the grand endeavour in its construction, preparation, furnishing, or field work. People were confused and slow to leave, some even refused to obey the directive of the highest order at first. It was the first time the populace hesitated to obey the orders of its young King, many could not believe that the order had really come from their ruler, and in the end the army had to be deployed to go searching house to house, street to street, and neighbourhood to neighbourhood. But the newly built city was so beautiful that there were a few unusual cases of desertion from the military; the deserters did not want to leave the city and sought hiding places in cellars and attics. Umbras learned about these dramatic events at the same time as the Emperor, when, with his ears covered so as not to hear his own words, he was reading the messages of the commanders and officers, who personally had to search everything once more in order to catch the deserters from their own units. During that time Umbras was also reading to Your Most Exalted Majesty scrolls of letters arriving from other parts of our vast empire. They were written by the administrators of various districts and regions, and the gist of them was that the people of the whole land were waiting with bated breath, expecting a wise explanation from their Emperor and King to make sense of such an unexpected change, which had turned a newly created province built with unprecedented enthusiasm, but also with painful callouses and the sweat of the brow of the majority of the population, into an abandoned world without people.

Umbras was hoping, naively and immodestly, that he would be the one to whom the Emperor of the Land and King of Its People would dictate the words of an insightful explanation that would convince the populace of the empire anew and more strongly than ever of the wisdom of their ruler. But instead of such a message came the news which shocked, and for a time also paralysed, the entire country: bad news about how the buildings of the new city and the surrounding settlements on the opposite bank of the river Plamur and the other side of the Iklabe mountain range had collapsed under the forces of an unprecedented earthquake, which buried in the rubble the remaining brave army commanders who were rounding up the hidden deserters. From the messages of higher officials and commanders of various provinces that Umbras read to Your Most Exalted Majesty in the days that followed, it became clear that our empire had turned into a hotbed of all kinds of rumours and presuppositions. An idea spread among the people that the Emperor of the Land and King of Its People, who enjoyed special favour with the Almighty Creator and Fair Judge, had received a warning in a dream, in which he was told about the imminent earthquake, and thus he had ordered the province to be evacuated. At the same time, there were whispers that it was a warning for the Emperor of the Land and King of Its People, a reproachful finger of the Almighty Creator himself, angered by the young ruler's decision to build a beautiful city resembling the world of bliss into which the Fair Judge only lets the cleanest souls from among the departed.

Besides these speculations, the empire also thrived on other unverified reports, particularly ones that spoke of a terrible illness similar to the most contagious blue cholera, which even the slightest breeze could carry from the bodies of the men who had died in the ruins of the destroyed Plamikia. There was talk of dozens of dead imperial court officials who had been sent to tabulate the extent of the damage and were smitten by the contagion, and about healers who had betrayed the oath of their guild to fight for the life of every person and refused to set foot on the bridge over the river Plamur even under the threat of imprisonment, because they knew that what awaited them on the opposite bank of the river was a slow but certain death after untold suffering. In the end, these rumours proved to be true; they were confirmed by another directive of the highest order, which Umbras took down several days later, and which the third-level court scribes immediately copied dozens upon dozens of times, so that it could be disseminated across the whole empire as quickly as possible. The Emperor of the Land and King of Its People forbade, under penalty of death, any type of crossing of the river Plamur, whether on dry land across the bridge, or on water in any kind of vessel or without one. The reason was an unknown and therefore incurable illness, which had spread across Plamikia after the devastating earthquake. Anyone who learned of someone crossing the river Plamur or the Iklabe mountain range, without regard for the direction of travel, would have to inform the nearest military commander. After finishing the scroll with this directive of the highest order, Umbras took down two more decrees. In the first one, the Emperor of the Land and King of Its People informed his higher officials and the commanders of the various provinces that he was disbanding Plamikia province and removing the territory on which it was located from his empire. In the next decree he instructed the commanders of the military units on how to deal with those who disobeyed the aforementioned directive of the highest order. If the guilty party was headed towards the territories where Plamikia province used to be, he was to be detained and sentenced; if he was coming from those territories, he was to be killed on the spot by shots from a longbow or a crossbow, from a distance of at least twenty paces. From this distance the body was to be guarded for a minimum of seven days, so that no person would come near it, nor dogs, cats, livestock, or other farm animals, after which time the body was to be burned on the spot. When Your Most Exalted Majesty was speaking the words of this decree, blindfolded Umbras could hear sadness in the melody of the Emperor's voice; the tone of the King's speech was uncertain, as with someone who has doubts about the correctness of his actions. It was the first time the Emperor of the Land and King of Its People was ordering someone to be killed, and although he knew that the measure was necessary to prevent contagion, therefore saving a great number of other lives, he felt sorry for the person who would be subject to this decree, as much as for the person who would have to follow the decree, but, most of all, for the person handing down the decree.

Although many feelings of anger, loss, and the futility of earthly matters made Your Most Exalted Majesty's heart race in those days, Umbras admired your decisiveness and judgement. But decisiveness was just one drop in the vessel of your wisdom, others were the art of listening to others, prudence in choosing a path, speed of decision making, the ability to tell the small from the big, the essential from the insignificant, but, most importantly, equanimity of mind and spirit in accepting the blows of fate, which undoubtedly stemmed from deference to the Almighty Creator and Fair Judge. A ruler is not made great by his victories but by his defeats, says a song in Pte, the language of the people from the South.

The next day Umbras took down an edict for the chief royal builder, in which the Emperor of the Land and King of Its People ordered the newly built bridge over the river Plamur to be torn down, and all the roads leading north towards the territory of the former Plamikia province to be blocked. This work was to be carried out in cooperation with the commanders of the relevant military units, because the military was to oversee the workmen to prevent any attempt to set foot on the opposite bank of the river or the other side of the mountain range. Thus in the two--hundred-and-seventeenth year after the destructive flood, the land of fertile green plains in the north became even more inaccessible than it was before Your Most Exalted Majesty had discovered it on his expedition.

A short time later—only a few days may have passed—scrolls with messages from commanders of the loyal Imperial Guard started to arrive from various provinces and districts of the empire. They were informing you that people had started to disappear all over the country; loving fathers had disappeared from their families, faithful wives from their husbands, caring daughters from their infirm parents. Umbras read these papyri to Your Most Exalted Majesty with his ears plugged with thin scribe's mud, so that he could not hear the detailed and precise lists of the missing people from all walks of life, at the end of which there was usually a note that the secret Imperial Guard had no information about the fate of these people. Later, when the disappearance of people became part of everyday life in the country, the commanders showed ever-increasing despair. They admitted that they were unable to explain what was going on in their districts. The most observant ones, who were frequently also the most experienced and had served in the secret Imperial Guard for many years, pointed out that all the missing people were exemplary servants of the Law of Princess Hordona, the most ethical and virtuous of citizens; they were honest merchants who had never been accused of deception, exemplary fathers who had fully engaged in raising their progeny, and virtuous wives who had never made a single gesture that would suggest a desire to charm and seduce another man.

In his replies, the Emperor of the Land and King of Its People urged the secret Imperial Guard to be vigilant and alert, but now, when one half of Umbras's lungs is about to take its last breath and the other is already exhaling for the last time, he can admit that already back then, when he was sitting in front of his ruler with a quill in his hand and writing down these replies on scrolls, it surprised him that Your Most Exalted Majesty had no clear and detailed plan to address the plague that was troubling our empire. Umbras has a suspicion and he wants to share it with the listeners of these words organised into lines; he is bold enough to hope that first and foremost among them will be the Emperor of the Land and King of Its People, followed by the ears of those listening to the reader who will pick up this scroll many years from now, when Umbras's name will have been forgotten dozens of times over and his bones will have long turned to dust.

Reports of the disappearances of people were reaching Umbras not only via the scrolls that he was reading to Your Most Exalted Majesty, but also in oral form from his friends and family. When he was on one of his rare visits at his father Uraten and mother Distrimoda's house, they were unable to speak about anything else, they just cried in sympathy over the fate of those who had been lost, but even more so over the fate of their relatives, orphaned children, abandoned wives and husbands. The eyes of the parents and neighbours who saw Umbras coming to visit were looking up to him with hope; after all, he spent his days among the higher dignitaries in the imperial palace, he was close to the ruler himself, he was able to look him in the face, therefore he must have been able to report on what was going on and ask the Emperor of the Land and King of Its People for help. It is only now that Umbras understands that even the hopelessness of orphans and the helplessness of abandoned old men had their purpose, their place, because they opened the gates of charity, sympathy, and kindness, they allowed the good to come forth from within people, particularly in those decisive times of separating the wheat from the chaff.

Your Most Exalted Majesty, Umbras clasps his hands together in prayer to the Almighty Creator and Fair Judge, asking him that each of your subjects admire and trust you the way Umbras admires and trusts you as he humbly writes the lines of this scroll in the dark and dampness. He admired you and trusted you just as much during the times he is attempting to document. Umbras is now an old man ready to hand over half his body to cadaver worms, because they will take the other half themselves; his expectations and hopes have shrunk to the size of a single flax seed, which hides the desire for Your Most Exalted Majesty not to doubt that the humble servant was then and is now the most loyal of all the servants of the Emperor of the Land and King of Its People. Which is precisely why one day, when Umbras finished writing another secret message to one of the commanders or secretaries, before Your Most Exalted Majesty summoned the imperial servant to untie the scarf covering Umbras's eyes, your humble servant and admirer dared to speak, because for several days he had been burning with the desire to reveal to his Emperor of the Land and King of Its People the great secret that bound the scribes' guild. With utmost deference, Umbras asked his ruler to grant him a short moment of his precious time, which should have been devoted to the well-being of the land and the happiness of its people, and Your Most Exalted Majesty benevolently indulged his scribe. Umbras opened by saying that in those difficult times he admired above all the prudence and wisdom of his ruler, who had not let himself stray from the path because of unexpected events, which showed a penetrating mind and clear judgement, as well as unshakeable will and perseverance. Umbras wanted to continue, because for days he had been thinking about the words to describe truthfully the virtues of his ruler, but a light shadow of displeasure on the Emperor's face and a dismissive motion of the royal right hand, neither of which the blindfolded scribe could have seen, indicated to him that he should go on to the thing he was trying to say. Umbras, who had been sitting on the scribe's stool, threw himself face-down on the ground, his forehead touching the cold green marble, which—although constantly walked on—still added grandeur to the ruler's day chamber, and in that deferential position the poor scribe asked, in the name of all the scribes of the land, regardless of their position or rank, for forgiveness for the lie which they had been peddling for ages to the Emperor as well as the land and to the King as well as its people. The stern voice of Your Most Exalted Majesty ordered Umbras to continue, and, sobbing, Umbras admitted that even when he was blind-folded so that he could not see what his quill was writing, he was still aware of and knew everything that was being dictated to him. At first Your Most Exalted Majesty did not believe it, so you asked the blindfolded Umbras to read a scroll that was still spread out on the counter, at which point the crying scribe explained that the issue was not reading while blindfolded, because no one could manage such a feat, but it was listening, since a dictated word went from the scribe's ears to his mind, and only from there did it move to the fingers which were holding the quill. There was no direct connection between the ear and the hand, they were connected through the mind which resided in the head, and which was only a step away from memory, so there was no point in blindfolding a scribe, because he learned the contents of what he was recording beforehand via his own hearing, and he stored it in his memory, which Umbras, with his face and body still lying on the cold marble and his eyes blindfolded, proved by repeating the contents of the secret message he had written down a moment earlier. The imperial scribe fell silent, only his occasional sobs carrying through the hall, but then the echo of the approaching steps of Your Most Exalted Majesty reached his ears. Umbras expected that at any moment he would hear the high-pitched dragging sound of his young ruler's dagger being pulled out of its scabbard in order to end the life of the unworthy servant, because the humble scribe had expected just such a punishment as he pondered his confession for several days, but he was unable to continue living a lie when every day he came face to face with so much magnificence, courage, and prudence in the Emperor of the Land and King of Its People. But instead of fair punishment, Your Most Exalted Majesty nobly decided to gift his servant his life, kneel, and untie the scarf on his head. The gazes of the ruler and his servant met for a brief moment, and for the latter of the two, this brief moment became a source of strength in the hard life that was about to begin for him. Umbras saw a flash of delight in the eyes of his young sovereign which he has never forgotten, and even now he can recall it from his memory completely clearly, although he must admit that the two halves that form the inside of a human head do not serve him reliably any more, since one of them is about to give over to the sleep of death, and the other gave over to it long ago. I knew that you were righteous, the Emperor of the Land and King of Its People said to his unworthy servant Umbras, who, encouraged by his ruler's words that washed over him like a wave of happiness and joy, immediately revealed that the writers' guild was peddling a similar lie about the act of reading, since the custom of plugging the ears with thin scribe's mud was completely superfluous and ineffective, because even though the person reading could not hear his own words, he took them in through his eyes as they were going over the lines. His sight would put the words into his mind, and only then would come the command to the tongue and lips to speak, to read.

I knew that you were righteous—those words were the highest recognition the humble servant Umbras could receive from his ruler. Umbras immersed himself in the cloud of happiness and joy, because he had been praised by his sovereign, the man for whom he had the utmost respect and whose every deed and every decision he admired, since in Umbras's eyes, Your Most Exalted Majesty was the most exalted of all the emperors our land had ever seen, and the most insightful of all the kings the Almighty Creator had bestowed upon its people. The humble servant, whose heart and mind were bathing in the refreshing pool of delighted joy, received an order from his Emperor of the Land and King of Its People to take down another scroll. It was a commanding decree intended for all scribes, imperial and public, military and municipal, ordering them to end immediately the shameful practice of pretending that if they were writing blindfolded they did not know the content of the words they had written, and if they were reading with their ears plugged they did not know the sentences they had read. Under threat of imprisonment, the scribes were forbidden to perpetuate any other lies on dignitaries, the military, or the public, including inaccurate or incomplete writing or reading. Your Most Exalted Majesty then clearly defined the role and position of the scribe and reader—to be the one who does not interfere, even though he stands in the middle. He does not interfere, meaning he does not change that which is being dictated or has been written, and he is the intermediary between two people who are talking to one another by means of a scroll. A reader should be eyes following the lines and lips speaking what comes before the eyes; a scribe should be ears listening to words and fingers holding a quill, which records those words verbatim. Recording the will of Your Most Exalted Majesty, Umbras was ashamed to remember his beginnings in the scribe's stand at the market in the lower town, where he often dulled the indignation of the words of the people who dictated their letters to him. After the new commanding decree was issued, no scribe would be able to resort to anything like that.

In the two-hundred-and-eighteenth year after the destructive flood, Umbras, the son of his father Uraten and his mother Distrimoda, read to the Emperor of the Land and King of Its People the first of many nearly identical entreaties. This one had been dictated by the council of wise men and all the citizens of one of the small towns in the interior—it could have been Ol-ar Roama or Alo-ar Roan, your humble servant over the grave, half of whose memory is going and the other half has already gone to the other world, honestly cannot remember, but in the end it does not really matter, because if the first plea came from the men and women of Ol-ar Roama, soon another, very similar one would have come from the people of Alo-ar Roan. Messengers all over the land brought scrolls, in which the citizens were turning to the Emperor of the Land and King of Its People, desperate, frightened, and crushed by the scale of the disappearances of people, as if some mysterious dark force were sucking out our empire—those exact words were written in several of the pleas, and it seemed that way to Umbras as well, since priests were performing services all over the land, asking the Almighty Creator and Fair Judge to rid our land of this inexplicable plague which raged among the men and women, young and old, rich and poor, craftsmen and military, with the destructive power of the most contagious blue cholera; there was no family which had been spared by this plague. The land was asking its Emperor and the people were asking their King for appropriate protection and effective help.

Another way to interpret the lines of several of these pleas could be that the people were asking their ruler to order an end to the kidnappings that were being organised by one of the imperial agencies or one of the royal administrators, and in three or four scrolls they were directly urging Your Most Exalted Majesty to be merciful and order the

release of their fellow citizens from prison, since the secret
Imperial Guard or the military had undoubtedly arrested
them by mistake; it must have been some inexplicable mis-
understanding because they were the best of the best. In
one case they offered as proof the honesty of a merchant,
in another the work ethic of a craftsman, who was also an
exemplary father of six children, and in another the obedi-
ence of a disappeared daughter, who took exceptional care
of her infirm father. Around the time the first pleas were
arriving, Umbras was reading his ruler messages from the
commanders of the secret Imperial Guard, in which they
wrote that they suspected the military was behind the disappearances, and messages from the military district leaders,
who suspected the secret Imperial Guard was behind the
kidnappings. Your Most Exalted Majesty did not pay much
attention to these suspicions, which Umbras really appre-
ciated, because it meant that the Emperor of the Land and
King of Its People trusted his army as well as the secret
Imperial Guard, which was undoubtedly another mark of
a good ruler. In contrast, a suspicious nature is the hallmark
of a weak, indecisive, or deranged ruler, who over time turns
into a palace fool. At the age when half of Umbras's hair has
already fallen out, and the other half is getting ready for its
post-mortem growth, this humble servant of his ruler can
open the gates of his imagination and wonder what things
would be like if a man less talented and less enlightened
had been the Emperor of the Land and King of Its People.
If it so happened that fate had been inebriated by young
wine or was under the influence of the intoxicating smoke

of a forbidden pipe, and it had made another person the ruler, he would certainly have been a bad emperor or king, because in a situation like the one Umbras is describing, he would have been suspicious, he would have thought about the fact that at any given moment, for reasons unknown, several commanders of the military or the secret Imperial Guard could have stopped abiding by the best interest of their kingdom and the orders of their emperor and advanced their own secret plans instead. Such a possibility probably did not even cross Your Most Exalted Majesty's mind. Therefore, your humble imperial scribe was all the more surprised by how much attention Your Most Exalted Majesty was paying to one unsubstantiated claim that the military was taking the kidnapped people into the forbidden territory by the river Plamur and throwing them into the water. In response, the Emperor of the Land and King of Its People dictated, by means of his loyal scribe, a secret message to the commanders of the northern military districts in which he ordered even stricter patrolling of the border.

On one cold morning during the rainy season, when endless rain was beating down on the roofs of the imperial palace and the raindrops were knocking the last leaves off the trees, Umbras was awakened early in the morning by sharp motions in his bowels. An unpleasant dampness pervaded the scribes' bedroom, making its way into the bedding, clothing, even human skin; it had seeped into Umbras's bones and enveloped his internal organs; he felt as though he had been penetrated by an invisible cold fog.

He threw the thickest bearskin cloak over his shoulders, and at the hour on the border between late night and early morning, he walked briskly down the empty corridors of the lower palace towards the latrines for higher-level servants. All of a sudden, a hulking figure in a dark cloak appeared from behind a column, crossing his path, its face masked with a scarf, revealing only the whites of its ominously gleaming eyes. Before Umbras could turn around and run, before he could call for help, the strong arms of another person grabbed him from behind, and a third man tied his hands with a sturdy rope which cut into his flesh, while the attacker in the black cloak forced the scribe's mouth open and shoved a wooden stopper into it, which Umbras was unable to spit out because there was nowhere to spit, since he had been quickly gagged with a thick rag. Then the arms picked up Umbras with no extra effort and shoved him into a large sack, which one of the men easily threw over his shoulder. They were strong men and their movements attested to the fact that it was not their first or second time doing this, but they had already repeated these actions dozens upon dozens of times. The men set out with their load, which was an appropriate term for Umbras at that moment. Seven times he heard the creaking of hinges when they went through doors, three times there was the echo of steps crossing a courtyard, then Umbras's head bounced up and down because the men were carrying him down a very long stairwell. Shame and a sense of decency do not permit the humble servant to describe how his full bowels, further weakened by great fear, had emptied their contents, which first spilled across Umbras's back toward his head, since in the sack his head was down and his rear end was up, and when the odour and the wetness leaked through the linen sack, the kidnappers got so angry that several swear words and insults burst forth from their lips, directed at Umbras, who recognised them as Pte, and their meanings were wild boar, polecat, stench, mud, and coward.

Umbras apologises for having tainted the hearing of the Emperor of the Land and King of Its People with his words, and he promises that he will not describe his great suffering in detail and length, so as not to offend the sensibilities of Your Most Exalted Majesty, because in a scroll meant for the ruler it is not appropriate to record words that describe all the filth, hunger, thirst, pain, fear, and despair which became Umbras's daily lot. Since this humble servant knows how busy with his duties and exhausted by pressing matters the Emperor of the Land and King of Its People was during that time, Umbras dares to presume that Your Most Exalted Majesty did not have full information about the ways, means, and instruments by which that grandiose plan was being carried out, but then, the sacrifices connected to making it a reality are but pearls that increase its lustre.

As Umbras came to find out, the overfilled cell into which his mysterious kidnappers had thrown him was located in the jail of the White Fortress, under the southern stables, between the three-sided cistern and the archery training grounds. In cells meant for half a dozen prisoners, four times that number of men were crammed in, so that in order for six of them to get some sleep on the narrow cots made of unfinished wood, eighteen had to stand. Since the prison was located deep underground, it was impossible to keep track of the passage of time based on sunlight or moonlight, and the regular beating of the gong from the courtyard of the third palace could not be heard there either, therefore the prisoners had to count the time for swapping who was sleeping. One of them was always counting dozens of dozens in a whisper, and when he reached the end, time was up for the ones lying down; they would get up and free the meagre cots for others. The ones who were not lying down took turns in a similar manner, because in order for six to move their bones with a few slow steps, the rest had to press up against the damp and mouldy walls of the cell. Similar shifts had to be taken for eating, because in order for half the men to be at least somewhat satiated by the little bit of thin, over-salted porridge which the jailers stuck under the bars, the other half had to give up their share entirely, and at the next distribution of porridge they would switch roles, and the ones who had been afforded a few bites in their mouths before would now go hungry. Everything that went on in the cell happened under the constant supervision of the jailers; a pair of them watched the prisoners through one of the small windows drilled into the walls. These jailers never said a word to the prisoners, but they were ever present, and once in a while their eyes would flash in the dim torchlight.

It is important to note that, just like him, not one of Umbras's co-sufferers crammed into the cell was aware of a specific crime or transgression against the words of the Law of Princess Hordona for which he should have been imprisoned or tried, though several regretted not having lived a more virtuous, selfless, or productive life. The men with whom Umbras shared his suffering displayed an uncommon willingness and desire to make sacrifices for one another. Even though they had not known each other before their imprisonment, they unselfishly lent their cloaks and shoes to protect the most vulnerable from the cold, they gave up their one daily meal if they saw that someone had greater need of it, they got up from the narrow cot before their time was up if they thought that someone else's body had a greater need to lie down than their own. This solidarity made the physical suffering of Your Most Exalted Majesty's servant more bearable, but at the same time it increased the hardship on his soul. Poor, sinful Umbras, half of whose face is stiffening with rigor mortis and the other half has already succumbed to decomposition, confesses to his ruler that he alone among the men imprisoned in the jail cell did not resist the great temptation of tiny selfish acts. Although he knows that it is too late for remorse, he is sincerely sorry in front of the Almighty Creator and Fair Judge, and no less so in front of the Emperor of the Land and King of Its People, that whenever the opportunity presented itself he remained on the cot longer than was his due, feigning weakness, and when he got the chance to walk in the cell, he took up precious space that others had as much right to as he did with his excessively long steps, and whenever it was his turn to count time, he never counted all the dozens of dozens, thus intentionally shortening the resting time of his fellow inmates, because he knew that the sooner they got up from the wooden cot, the sooner it would be available for him. But Umbras's selfish thoughtlessness and disregard for the suffering of others were most evident in the division of food and water. While others were offering one another the first turn to drink from the small pitcher, he pounced on the water and insatiably gulped down many more sips than belonged to him, and the same was true when cold porridge was being divvied up in the cell— Umbras was the only one to stick both his hands into the bowl so that he would pick up twice as much as the others on his grubby fingers. His fellow inmates watched the poor scribe with sympathy, but their compassion only humiliated and irritated him; more than that, it spurred him towards new and further expressions of inconsiderate selfishness.

Miserable Umbras now understands the higher purpose of his and his companions' imprisonment, he understands that suffering can be a wellspring that waters the sprouting seeds of goodness, pain can become a cleansing fire that rids a person of his faults and sins, and even though suffering weakens a person's body, it strengthens his mind. Unfortunately, none of that happened in the case of the poor imperial scribe. The men with whom he was sharing the narrow space enclosed by the damp, rough walls were concealing holy souls in their bodies, and they were sure to have already found favour in their present life with the Emperor of the Land and King of Its People, as well as with the Almighty Creator and Fair Judge. When they clasped their hands together for morning and evening prayers, even though they did not know whether the sun was really rising or setting, when they searched for a little bit of space to be able to kneel, Umbras saw so much devout faith and humble hope in their eyes that it made him grit his teeth in shame and fear of his own shallowness and malice.

After some time—Umbras is unable to describe this period with a number of days, because in the semi-darkness of the jail it is impossible to tell whether a day is dawning after the night or dusk is setting after the day—the dungeon gradually emptied. It seemed to Umbras that the first inmates to be led out of the dungeon were the bravest and most unselfish ones, but soon afterwards the rest were released, since all Umbras's co-sufferers were as brave and unselfish as could be, but before the cell emptied completely, the guards brought in new prisoners, so the poor scribe was not left alone. Umbras asked each of the poor souls who was thrown into the cell the reason for their imprisonment, but the answer was always the same: I do not know why I am here, it must be a mistake and I will be released soon, because I have spent my whole life trying to follow the commandments of the Almighty Creator and Fair Judge, and the words of the Law of Princess Hordona. All the men confirmed that they had been dragged away in secret and without witnesses, either at night or from a remote place. At first they also thought that they had been attacked by bandits or marauding foreigners, but they quickly became persuaded that some powerful office of our land was behind their kidnapping. Umbras apologises to Your Most Exalted Majesty for the words he dared to use, but he did so only to suggest that the men gathered in the dark cells under the southern stables had an inkling of some of the intentions, even though the whole breadth, depth, and height of the great plan could only have been clear to the Emperor of the Land and King of Its People. The imprisoned men could only know as much as a guardian of a tower knows about his surroundings in the thick morning fog. They were hoping for a quick release, but even if capital punishment befell them, they were prepared to submit without despair or fear, because they believed in the mercy of the Fair Judge. Overall, they were people similar in their virtues to those who had been in the cell with Umbras before. But as women from the South would say, Umbras had an advantage in a disadvantage over the new prisoners, in that he already knew how life in prison worked, so he completely naturally took on the role of leader or commander, or, more precisely, he usurped this position, and the rest let him have it without grumbling, with deference, and perhaps also with some apathy. Umbras decided the portions of water and porridge, he ordered who could lie down and when, all the while prioritising his own belly and his own back. The men always accepted his decisions, not because they feared the strength of his arms, since several of them were incomparably stronger, their arms having been strengthened by physical labour and not by holding a scribe's quill, but because of their yielding nature, and perhaps also because Umbras veiled his decisions, which always brought him at least a slight benefit, in explanations that seemed to be helping those who were the most exhausted or suffering the greatest hardship. In spite of the sharp wits and keen judgement of Umbras's fellow inmates, their pure hearts did not allow them to discover his deceit, thanks to which he ended up being the one lying down the longest, drinking and eating the most, walking in the sturdiest shoes, and covered in the warmest clothing acquired from one of his co-sufferers, since Umbras's bearskin cloak had been lost during his kidnapping.

After some time, the guards started to take away men from this group as well, beginning with the most unselfish and most merciful ones, until the cell was almost empty again, which opened up space for new prisoners, and the cell quickly filled up. The whole process was repeated a dozen or a dozen-and-a-half times. Then, all of a sudden, Umbras remained alone; no new prisoner showed up. The hubbub from the passageway where other similar cells must have been was slowly decreasing as well. The glistening eyes disappeared from the openings in the walls through which the prisoners had been constantly observed by the watchful gaze of the guards, and one day, or perhaps one night, sharp hammer blows closed the openings from the other side with large wooden plugs. An endless period of solitude began for Umbras, without so much as a single word from a human mouth for the longest part of his life, about which he has nothing to write, except that he occasionally yelled at the hands that shoved a bowl of porridge or a pitcher of water under the bars, but there was never an answer, therefore the only words originating in human mouths were the muffled fragments of sentences he overheard being exchanged by unknown jailers in the passageways. For uncountable days—truly uncountable, because in the constant darkness of a dungeon it is not possible to count days, therefore their count does not exist—the only company Umbras had were rats, bugs, and centipedes, which in that underground world suffered as much as he, the former scribe and reader to the Emperor of the Land and King of Its People. Life went on in the courtyards of the imperial palace, people passed one another on the streets and squares, harvests ripened in the fields, but Umbras remained outside time, outside any happenings or change. But that was just a false illusion caused by solitude, which can have an effect like opium on the human mind, clouding one's judgement, because the opposite was true, and the thing that was constantly moving in the cell was Umbras himself; his body was moving towards its end, so that now, the son of his father Uraten and his mother Distrimoda can honestly say that half of him is already dead, and the other half never lived. For one cannot call living the time spent on a narrow cot with thoughts that have completely erased the present, with senses the mind has commanded not to perceive the gentle rustling of a centipede's legs moving or the reflections of the torchlight from a passing guard, because Umbras had trained his whole inner being to keep returning to the past; one by one he re-examined every day of his life, in his memory he went back to every situation and circumstance he had lived through. Just as years ago reality had inscribed itself into his memory, now individual memories were turning into events that Umbras was reliving, but this time with a rational detachment; he judged his actions, labelled his emotions, and searched for connections, causes, and effects between the events. First, his whole childhood ran through his head—he used to play with his mother Distrimoda, he used to listen to fairy tales his father Uraten told him, he studied to be a scribe, he sat in his scribe's stand at the market in the lower town, then he was summoned to the palace in order to become scribe and reader to the Emperor of the Land and King of Its People, he recorded decrees for dignitaries, read messages arriving from all corners of the land, and finally he became witness to the most magnificent and grandiose plan in all of history written after the destructive flood. The more Umbras's body wasted away in the dungeon, the more his mind opened up, as if approaching death were giving him back his reason, so that during the careful examination of his past days, the scribe came to understand the meaning of what had gone on around him; therefore, today he looks with undying respect upon the Emperor of the Land and King of Its People, upon that unique maker and discoverer of the greatest idea that has ever been born in a person's mind.

Gradually, the Emperor of the Land and King of Its People took on a crucial role in Umbras's reminiscences. He had assumed the throne as a young man; he was not satisfied with his empire, he wanted the people living in it to be better and happier, and although he was the ruler, he was not able to make it happen, therefore he escaped the reality of the world in nature, where he did not encounter villainy and treachery; he became an avid hunter, and on one hunt he discovered a vast fertile plain across the wild torrent of the river Plamur and over the cliffs of the Iklabe mountain range, and he named it Plamikia. In Plamikia, the Emperor's dream could turn into a royal plan; at a cost of great sacrifices he had a beautiful city with surrounding farm settlements built there, and when the city was built he issued a directive of the highest order recalling all the builders, workers, craftsmen, and administrators, that is, everyone who had had a hand in the grand endeavour; he let the news of a terrible earthquake spread, followed by an untreatable epidemic, therefore it was necessary to cut off all roads to Plamikia, but the earthquake and epidemic were just fabrications, a justification, an explanation for why no one could enter the new province; yet they still entered, in greatest secrecy many righteous and honourable men headed that way, noble and virtuous women, all of them kidnapped from an empire where evil reigned and taken to a new world which was being created according to the grandiose plan of the young ruler. The final test in which these chosen ones were to prove their goodness and mercy was a short time spent suffering in the dark cells of the jail in the White Fortress, under the southern stables, between the three-sided cistern and the archery training ground; there the future residents of Plamikia were tormented by hunger, thirst, cold, and filth; unprompted they had to show consideration and kindness towards one another, so that after overcoming this last hurdle they could go directly to the new world, open only to the best of the best. Umbras bends his old back in deference, bowing before this plan of Your Most Exalted Majesty, even though he himself did not pass his final test; he may have been the only person designated for life in the bliss of Plamikia who had failed; right before the finish line he did not measure up, therefore he stayed imprisoned in a dungeon, no longer belonging to either of the worlds outside; he was too good for one, and not good enough for the other.

Umbras was locked up in his damp and cold cell, and in his mind dulled by age and his limited imagination he is attempting to imagine what went on around the empire after the last of the good people had been spirited away, when those who had remained in the city streets and rural settlements were some of the worse and the worst, the damned, who did not have the right to the bliss of Plamikia. These poor souls were no longer exposed to the purifying influence of the good people, thus life in the empire must have started to deteriorate rapidly; there were more murders, robberies, thefts; adultery spread, as did property fraud, quarrels, insults, gossip; people visited the temples less and they neglected their prayers; the whole country was subject to the proliferation of evil in both its forms, crimes of burning malice as well as crimes of smouldering malice. People started to rebel, even against the Emperor of the Land and King of Its People; some dared to blame him for not preventing the kidnapping of their loved ones, others went so far as to accuse him of orchestrating those kidnappings by means of his secret Imperial Guard. After the verbal attacks came assaults on military personnel and fortresses, and finally—here Umbras apologises deeply to Your Most Exalted Majesty for his assumptions—there was a general uprising that culminated in an attack on the imperial palace. At this point, Umbras's imagination couples with the meagre evidence that makes its way into his cell. His hearing, weakened by old age, has recently caught a conversation between two excited guards about the fact that the palace has been surrounded. And just a little while ago, a frightened scream announced that the rebels have attacked the eastern citadel; another scream answered, saying that the western fortress was already in flames. Umbras has no doubt that this too was part of the wisest and bravest plan to have ever been born in a human mind since the destructive flood, given that through this rebellion, this civil war that has taken hold of the whole empire and is consuming it from within like an insatiable intestinal parasite, leading it towards destruction, towards mutual annihilation of all the bad people, evil will destroy evil, it will be eradicated together with those who were its carriers, so that only untainted goodness will remain, hidden in safety across the wild torrent of the river Plamur and over the inaccessible peaks of the Iklabe mountain range. Umbras, the son of his father Uraten and his mother Distrimoda, is old and decrepit; part of his soul dreams of nothing but eternal rest, while the other part is already floating above the green plains of Plamikia, and the words of the last prayer of the former imperial scribe belong to Your Most Exalted Majesty. Umbras, shaking from coughing and chills, prays to the Almighty Creator and Fair Judge that in these critical moments, when the whole empire has split into a good half and an evil half, the Emperor of the Land and King of Its People may stand on the blessed side, on the other side of the mountain range, on the opposite bank of the river.